Running From Legs

and other stories

Other Five Star Titles
by Ed McBain:

Barking at Butterflies and Other Stories

Running From Legs

and other stories

Ed McBain
a.k.a. Evan Hunter

Five Star
Unity, Maine

Copyright © 2000 by Hui Corporation

This collection is a work of fiction. Names, characters, places, and incidents are either the product of the author's imagination, or, if real, used fictitiously.

Five Star First Edition Mystery Series.
Published in 2000 in conjunction with Teckno Books and Ed Gorman.

First Edition, Second Printing

Cover photograph by Dragica Dimitrijević-Hunter

The text of this edition is unabridged.

Set in 11 pt. Plantin.

Printed in the United States on permanent paper.

Library of Congress Cataloging-in-Publication Data

McBain, Ed, 1926–
    Running from Legs and other stories / by Ed McBain
a.k.a. Evan Hunter..
        p. cm.—(Five Star first edition mystery series)
    Contents: The interview—The fallen angel—The prisoner
—Terminal misunderstanding— The sharers—The couple
next door—The victim—But you know us—Running from
Legs—Happy New Year, Herbie—The last spin.
    ISBN 0-7862-2671-4 (hc : alk. paper)
    1. Detective and mystery stories, American. I. Title:
Running from Legs. II. Title. III. Series.
PS3515.U585 R86   2000
813'.54—dc21   00-034747

This, yet again, is for my wife

Dragica Dimitrijević-Hunter

Table of Contents

Introduction

Only one story in this collection was published under the pseudonym Ed McBain. That one was the title story, "Running From Legs," and it first saw the light of day in 1996. Most of the other stories all appeared under my own name, Evan Hunter. Three of the stories in this collection were *never* published anywhere before, under *either* name.

You may well ask why.

I will tell you why.

They were probably not good enough.

(I don't believe that for a moment.)

Because I am a master of suspense, or rather because *Ed McBain* is a master of suspense, I won't tell you which those three stories are until you're almost finished reading this little introduction. Instead, I will answer another question I feel certain is burning in your mind, and that is this: If only *one* story that follows was published under the Ed McBain pseudonym, why then does he get top billing on the cover and the title page of this book?

I will tell you why.

He is a better writer than Evan Hunter.

(I don't believe *that* for a moment, either.)

Otto Penzler, mystery connoisseur, maven of all crime mavens, insists that a crime story is any story that has a crime central to the plot. By his definition (and who would doubt such an expert?) "Running From Legs" is most definitely a crime story. He should know. He published it in an anthology called *Murder for Love*. But by his definition, "The Last Spin," which was first published in Manhunt in 1956 (the cover of the magazine bellowing "By the Author of *The Blackboard Jungle!*") and "The Prisoner," which came out the following year, and "The Interview," which was published in Playboy in 1971, are all crime stories as well and *should* have been published under the McBain name except that no one but my agent, my wife, and my mother (maybe) knew who Ed McBain was back then. Four out of eleven stories, however, do not a crime wave make and certainly do not constitute sufficient cause for headlining McBain over Hunter, do they? I mean, just turn the damn spotlight over to him that way? I mean, four out of *eleven?*

(Well, remember, *three* of those eleven were never published before now. Which means that *half* of the following stories are rightfully crime stories that fall in McBain's bailiwick. Four out of *eight,* right?)

It wasn't until a decade after the release of the film version of *The Blackboard Jungle* that I hit a so-called slick magazine with a short story. This was "The Fallen Angel," published in 1965 in the *Ladies Home Journal,* the same magazine that had serialized *The Blackboard Jungle* in 1954. Short story sales to *Playboy* followed in rapid succession—both "The Interview" and "The Sharers" in 1971, the aforementioned "Terminal Misunderstanding" in 1972. The byline on all these stories was Evan Hunter.

Which brings us back to the essential question.

Why does McBain get top billing here, huh?

I will tell you why.

I owe a lot to him.

He's kept me honest over the years.

If ever I begin to think I'm a "literary" writer, he looks me square in the eye and says, "Hey, come on up the precinct, pal."

If ever I begin to think my stories are too good for some simple-minded editor to appreciate, he says, "Come on, they're probably lousy."

(I don't believe that even when *he* says it.)

By now, I know you're wondering which of these three stories were too lousy to publish anywhere before this very instant. Well, you already have eight of the titles that *were* published, so a simple process of elimination should give you the three rejects. But to spare you the agony of any further excruciating suspense . . .

The envelopes, please.

And the losers are . . .

"The Couple Next Door."

"The Victim."

And . . .

Drum roll.

"But You Know Us."

By my count, two Hunters and a McBain, since "The Victim" is probably a crime story.

That gives us a total of six Hunters and only five McBains—but who's counting?

Now you know us.

Evan Hunter
Ed McBain
Weston, Connecticut

The Interview

Sir, ever since the Sardinian accident, you have refused to grant any interviews . . .

I had no desire to join the circus.

Yet you are not normally a man who shuns publicity.

Not normally, no. The matter on Sardinia, however, was blown up out of all proportion, and I saw no reason for adding fuel to the fire. I am a creator of motion pictures, not of sensational news stories for the press.

There are some "creators of motion pictures" who might have welcomed the sort of publicity the Sardinian . . .

Not I.

Yet you will admit the accident helped the gross of the film.

I am not responsible for the morbid curiosity of the American public.

Were you responsible for what happened in Sardinia?

On Sardinia. It's an island.

On Sardinia, if you will.

I was responsible only for directing a motion picture. Whatever else happened, happened.

You were there when it happened however . . .

I was there.

So certainly . . .

I choose not to discuss it.

The actors and technicians present at the time have had a great deal to say about the accident. Isn't there anything you'd like to refute or amend? Wouldn't you like to set the record straight?

10

The record is the film. My films are my record. Everything else is meaningless. Actors are beasts of burden and technicians are domestic servants, and refuting or amending anything either might care to utter would be a senseless waste of time.

Would you like to elaborate on that?

On what?

On the notion that actors . . .

It is not a notion, it is a simple fact. I have never met an intelligent actor. Well, let me correct that. I enjoyed working with only one actor in my entire career, and I still have a great deal of respect for him—or at least as much respect as I can possibly muster for anyone who pursues a profession that requires him to apply makeup to his face.

Did you use this actor in the picture you filmed on Sardinia?

No.

Why not? Given your respect for him . . .

I had no desire to donate fifty percent of the gross to his already swollen bank account.

Is that what he asked for?

At the time. It may have gone up to seventy-five percent by now, I'm sure I don't know. I have no intention of ever giving a ploughhorse or a team of oxen fifty percent of the gross of a motion picture I created.

If we understand you correctly . . .

You probably don't.

Why do you say that?

Only because I have never been quoted accurately in any publication, and I have no reason to believe your magazine will prove to be an exception.

Then why did you agree to the interview?

Because I would like to discuss my new project. I have a meeting tonight with a New York playwright who will be delivering the final draft of a screenplay upon which we have labored long and hard. I have every expectation that it will now meet my requirements. In which case, looking ahead to the future, this interview should appear in print shortly before the film is completed and ready for release. At least, I hope the timetable works out that way.

May we know who the playwright is?

I thought you were here to talk to me.

Well, yes, but . . .

It has been my observation that when Otto Preminger or Alfred Hitchcock or David Lean or even some of the fancy young *nouvelle vague* people give interviews, they rarely talk about anyone but themselves. That may be the one good notion any of them has ever contributed to the industry.

You sound as if you don't admire too many directors.

I admire some.

Would you care to name them?

I have admiration for Griffith, DeMille, Eisenstein, several others.

Why these men in particular?

They're all dead.

Are there no living directors you admire?

None.

None? It seems odd that a man known for his generosity would be so chary with praise for other acknowledged film artists.

Yes.

Yes, what?

Yes, it would seem odd, a distinct contradiction of personality. The fact remains that I consider every living director a threat, a challenge, and a competitor. There are only so many motion picture screens in the world, and there are thousands of films competing to fill those screens. If the latest Hitchcock thriller has them standing on line outside Radio City, the chances are they won't be standing on line outside my film up the street. The theory that an outstanding box-office hit helps *all* movies is sheer rubbish. The outstanding hit helps only itself. The other films suffer because no one wants to see them, they want to see only the big one, the champion, the one that has the line outside on the sidewalk. I try to make certain that all of my films generate the kind of excitement necessary to sustain a line on the sidewalk. And I resent the success of any film but my own.

Yet you have had some notable failures.

Failures are never notable. Besides, I do not consider any of my films failures.

Are we talking now about artistic failures or box-office failures?

I have never made an artistic failure. Some of my films were mildly disappointing at the box office. But not very many of them.

When the Sardinian film was ready to open last June . . .

July. It opened on the Fourth of July.

Yes, but before it opened, when . . .

That would have been June, yes. July is normally preceded by June.

There was speculation that the studio would not permit its showing.

Rubbish.

The rumors were unfounded? That the studio would suppress the film?

The film opened, didn't it? And was a tremendous success, I might add.

Some observers maintain that the success of the film was due only to the publicity given the Sardinian accident. Would you agree to that?

I'll ask *you* a question, young man. Suppose the accident on Sardinia had been related to a film called *The Beach Girl Meets Hell's Angels*, or some such piece of trash? Do you think

13

the attendant publicity would have insured the success of *that* film?

Perhaps not. But given your name and the stellar quality of . . .

You can stop after my name. Stars have nothing to do with any of my pictures. I could put a trained seal in one of my films, and people would come to see it. I could put you in a film, and people would come to see it.

Don't you believe that films are a collaborative effort?

Certainly not. I tell the script writer what I want, and he writes it. I tell the set designer what to give me, and he gives it to me. I tell the cameraman where to aim his camera and what lens to use. I tell the actors where to move and how to speak their lines. Does that sound collaborative to you? Besides, I resent the word "effort."

Why?

Because the word implies endeavor without success. You've tried to do something and you've failed. None of my films are "efforts." The word "effort' is like the word "ambitious." They both spell failure. Haven't you seen book jackets that proudly announce "This is So-and-So's most ambitious effort to date"? What does that mean to you? To me, it means the poor bastard has set his sights too high. And failed.

Are you afraid of failure?

I cannot abide it.

Do you believe the Sardinian film was a success? Artistically?

I told you earlier . . .

Yes, but many critics felt the editing of the film was erratic. That the sequences filmed before the drowning were inserted piece-meal into . . .

To begin with, whenever critics begin talking about editing or camera angles or dolly shots or anything technical, I instantly fall asleep. They haven't the faintest notion of what filmmaking is all about, and their pretentious chatter about the art may impress maiden ladies in Flushing Meadows, but it quite leaves me cold. In reality, *none* of them know what's going on either behind the camera or up there on the screen. Do you know what a film critic's sole requirement is? That he has seen a lot of movies, period. To my way of thinking, *that* qualifies him as an expert on popcorn, not on celluloid.

In any event, you were rather limited, were you not, in editing the final portion of the film?

Limited in what way?

In terms of the footage you needed to make the film a complete entity?

The film *was* a complete entity. Obviously, I could not include footage that did not exist. The girl drowned. That was a simple fact. We did not shoot the remainder of the film as originally planned, we *could* not. But the necessary script revisions were made on the spot—or rather in Rome. I flew to Rome to consult with an Italian screenwriter, who did the work I required.

He did not receive credit on the film.

He *asked* that his name be removed from the picture. I acceded to his wishes.

But not without a struggle.

There was no struggle.

It was reported that you struck him.

Nonsense.

On the Via Veneto.

The most violent thing I've ever done on the Via Veneto was to sip a Campari-soda outside Doney's.

Yet the newspapers . . .

The Roman press is notoriously inaccurate. In fact, there isn't a single good newspaper in all Italy.

But, sir, there was some dispute with the screen writer, wasn't

15

there? Surely, the stories about it couldn't all have been . . .

We had some words.

About what?

Oh my, we *must* pursue this deadly dull rot, mustn't we? All right, all right. It was *his* allegation that when he accepted the job, he had no idea the publicity surrounding the girl's death would achieve such hideous proportions. He claimed he did not wish his good Italian name—the little opportunist had written only one film prior to my hiring him, and that an Italian Western starring a second-rate American television actor—did not wish his name associated with a project that had even a *cloud* of suspicion hanging over it. Those were his exact words. Actually, quite the opposite was true. Which is why I resisted his idiotic ploy.

Quite the opposite? What do you mean?

Rather than trying to *avoid* the unfortunate publicity, I felt he was trying to capitalize on it. His move was really completely transparent, the pathetic little bastard. I finally let him have his way. I should have thought he'd be proud to have his name on one of my pictures. As an illuminating sidelight, I might add he did not return the five thousand dollars a week I'd paid for the typing he did. Apparently, my *money* did not have a similar "cloud of suspicion" hanging over it.

"Typing," did you say?

Typing. The ideas for changing the script to accommodate the . . . to allow for a more plausible resolution were all mine.

A resolution to accommodate the drowning?

To explain the absence of the girl in the remainder of the film. I'm reluctant to discuss this, because it has a ghoulish quality I frankly find distasteful. The girl *did,* after all, drown; she *did* die. But that was a simple fact, and we must not lose sight of another simple fact. However cold-blooded this may

16

sound, and I am well aware that it may be an unpopular observation, there had already been an expenditure of three million dollars on that film. Now I'm sure you know that leading players *have* taken ill, *have* suffered heart attacks, *have* died during the filming of other pictures. To my knowledge, such events have never caused a picture to halt production, and neither do I know of a single instance in which a film was entirely scrapped, solely because of the death of one of the leading players. Yet this was the very pressure being brought to bear on me immediately following the drowning, and indeed up to the time of the film's release.

Then the studio did try to suppress the film?

Well . . . at first, they only wanted to stop production. I refused. Later, when they saw the rough cut—this was when all the publicity had reached its peak—they sent in a team of strong-armed Executive Producers, and Production Chiefs, and what-have-you, all know-nothings with windy titles, who asked me to suppress the film. I told them exactly where to go. And then later on, when the film had been edited and scored, the same thing happened. I finally threatened suit. My contract called for a large percentage of the gross of that film, and I had no intention of allowing it to crumble unseen in the can.

You did not feel it was a breach of good taste to exhibit the film?

Certainly not. The girl met with an accident. The accident was no one's fault. She drowned. If a stunt man had died riding a horse over a cliff, would there have been all that brouhaha about releasing the film? I should say not.

But you must agree the circumstances surrounding the drowning . . .

The drowning was entirely accidental. We were shooting in shallow water.

The reports on the depth of the water vary from ten feet to forty feet. Neither of which might be considered shallow.

17

The water was no higher than her waist. And she was a tall girl. Five feet seven, I believe. Or eight. I'm not sure which.

Then how did she drown, sir?

I have no idea.

You were there, were you not?

I was on the camera barge, yes.

Then what happened?

I suppose we must set this to rest once and for all mustn't we? I would much rather discuss the present and/or the future, but apparently we cannot do that until we've dealt *ad nauseam* with the past.

As you wish, sir.

I wish the accident had never happened, sir, that is what *I* wish. I also wish I would not be pestered interminably about it. The Italian inquest determined that the drowning was entirely accidental. What was good enough for the Italian courts is damn well good enough for me. But there is no satisfying the American appetite for scandal, is there? Behind each accident or incident, however innocuous, however innocent, the American public *must* insist upon a plot, a conspiracy, a cabal. Nothing is permitted to be exactly what it appears to be. Mystery, intrigue must surround everything. Nonsense. Do you think any of us *wanted* that girl to drown? I've already told you how much money we'd spent on the picture before the accident. I would estimate now that the delay in completion, the cost of revisions, the necessity for bringing in a second girl to resolve the love story added at least a million dollars to the proposed budget. No one wanted the drowning. If for business reasons *alone,* no one wanted it.

Yet it happened.

It happened.

How?

The exact sequence of events is still unclear to me.

18

Your assistant director . . .

Yes.

Testified at the inquest . . .

Yes, yes.

That the girl pleaded not to go into the water.

The water was unusually cold that morning. There was nothing we could do about *that*. It was a simple fact. The light was perfect, we had our set-up, and we were prepared to shoot. Actors are like children, you know. If I had allowed her to balk at entering the water, the next thing I knew she'd have balked at walking across a lawn.

The writer of the original screenplay claims that the scene you were shooting that morning . . .

Where the girl swims in to the dock? What about it?

He claims he did not write that scene. He claims it was not in the original script.

Well, let him take that up with the Writers Guild.

Was it in the original script?

I have no idea. If there were no innovations during the shooting of a film . . . really, does anyone expect me to follow a script precisely? What then is my function as director? To shout "Louder" or "Softer" to an actor? Let the writers direct their own scripts, in that case. I assure you they would not get very far.

Was the scene an innovation? The scene in the water?

It might have been. I can't recall. If it was not in the original shooting script, as our Hollywood hack claims, then I suppose it was an innovation. By definition, yes, it would have been an innovation, isn't that so?

When was it added to the script?

I don't recall. I will sometimes get ideas for scenes the night before I shoot them. In which case, I will call in the technicians involved, and describe the set-up I will need the

19

next day, and I will have it in the morning. If there is additional dialogue involved, I'll see to it that the actors and the script girl have the necessary pages, and I'll ask the actors to study them overnight. If there is no additional dialogue . . .

Was there any dialogue in this scene?

No. The girl was merely required to swim in to the dock from a speedboat.

What do you do in such a case? In an added scene where there's no dialogue?

Oh, I'll usually take the actor aside and sketch in the scene for him. The gist of it. This was a particularly simple scene. She had only to dive over the side of the boat and swim in to the dock.

In shallow water?

Well, not so shallow that she was in any danger of hitting the bottom, if that's what you mean.

Then perhaps the estimates of the water's depth . . .

The water's depth was no problem for anyone who knew how to swim.

Did the girl know how to swim?

Of course she did. You certainly don't think I'd have allowed her to play a scene in water . . .

I merely wondered if she was a good swimmer or . . .

Adequate. She was neither Eleanor Holm nor Esther Williams, but the part didn't call for an Olympic champion, you know. She was an adequate swimmer.

When did you explain the gist of the scene to her?

That morning, I believe. If memory serves me . . . yes, I believe the idea came to me the night before, and I called in the people involved and told them what I would need the following morning. Which is when I explained the scene to her. At least, that's usually the way it works; I assume it worked the same way concerning this particular scene.

You explained that she would have to dive over the side of the boat and swim in to the dock?

Which is all she had to do.

Did she agree to do this?

Why, of course. She was an inexperienced little thing, this was her first film. Of course, she agreed. There was never any question of her not agreeing. She'd been modeling miniskirts or what-have-you for a teenage fashion magazine when I discovered her. This was an enormous opportunity for her, this film. Look at the people I surrounded her with! Do you know what we had to pay her leading man? Never mind. It still irritates me.

Is it true he threatened to walk off the picture after the girl drowned?

He has said so in countless publications across the length and breadth of the world. I'm surprised he hasn't erected a billboard on the moon, but I imagine he's petitioning NASA for the privilege this very moment.

But did he threaten to walk off?

He did. I could not allow it, of course. Neither would his contract allow it. An actor will sometimes be deluded into believing he is something more than a beast of the field. Even with today's largely independent production structure, the studio serves as a powerful steam roller flattening out life's annoying little bumps for any second-rate bit player who's ever seen his own huge face grinning down idiotically from a screen. The *real* head sometimes gets as big as the fantasy head up there. Walk off the picture? I'd have sued his socks from under him.

Why did he threaten to walk off?

We'd had difficulty from the start. I think he was searching for an excuse, and seized upon the girl's drowning as a ripe opportunity.

What sort of difficulty?

I do not believe I need comment on the reputation of the gentleman involved. It has been adequately publicized, even in the most austere family publications.

Is it true, then, that a romance was developing between him and the girl?

I have never yet worked on a film in which a romance did not develop between the girl and her leading man. That is a simple fact of motion picture production.

Was it a simple fact of this motion picture?

Unfortunately, yes.

Why do you say "unfortunately"?

The girl had a brilliant career ahead of her. I hated to see her in a position that . . . I hated to see her in such a vulnerable position.

Vulnerable?

The Italian press would have enjoyed nothing better than to link her romantically with someone of his reputation. I warned her against this repeatedly. We'd spent quite a lot of money grooming this girl, you know. Stardom may happen overnight, but it takes many days of preparation for that overnight event.

Did she heed your warnings?

She was very young.

Does that mean to say . . . ?

Nineteen, very young.

There were, of course, news stories of a developing romance between them. Despite your efforts.

Yes, despite them. Well.

Yes?

The young are susceptible. And yet, I warned her. Until the very end, I warned her. The night before she drowned, there was a large party at the hotel, given in my honor. We had seen the rushes on the shooting we'd done the day before, and we were all quite pleased, and I, of course, was more than ever certain that the girl was going to be a tremendous smash. That I had found someone, developed someone, who would most certainly become one of the screen's enduring personalities. No question about it. She had . . . she had a luminous quality that . . . it's impossible to explain this to a layman. There are people, however, who are bland, colorless, insipid, until you photograph them. And suddenly, the screen is illuminated with a life force that is positively blinding. She had that quality. And so I told her again, that night of the party, I took her aside, and we were drinking quietly, and I reminded her of what she had been, an unknown model for a juvenile fashion magazine, and of what she would most certainly become once this film was released, and I begged her not to throw this away on a silly flirtation with her leading man, a man of his reputation. The press was there, you know this was quite an occasion—I had met the host on the Riviera, oh years, ago, when I was doing another film, and this was something of a reunion. Well. Well, I suppose none of it matters quite, does it? She's dead. She drowned the next day.

What happened? At the party?

They managed to get some photographs of her. There is a long covered walk at the hotel, leading to the tower apartments that overlook the dock. The *paparazzi* got some pictures of the two of them in a somewhat, shall we say, compromising attitude. I tried to get the cameras, I struggled with one of the photographers . . .

Were these the photographs that were later published? After the accident?

Yes, yes. I knew even then, of course. When I failed to get those cameras, I knew her career was ruined. I knew that everything I'd done, all the careful work, the preparation—and all for *her*, you know, all to make the girl a star, a person in her own right—all of it was wasted. I took her to her room. I scolded her severely, and reminded her that makeup call was for six A.M.

What happened the next morning?

She came out to the barge at eight o'clock, made up and in costume. She was wearing a bikini, with a robe over it. It was quite a chilly day.

Was she behaving strangely?

Strangely? I don't know what you mean. She seemed thoroughly chastised, as well she might have. She sat alone and talked to no one. But aside from that, she seemed perfectly all right.

No animosity between you?

No, no. A bit of alienation perhaps. I had, after all, been furious with her the night before and had soundly reprimanded her. But I *am* a professional, you know, and I *did* have a scene to shoot. As I recall, I was quite courteous and friendly. When I saw she was chilled, in fact, I offered her my thermos.

Your thermos?

Yes. Tea. A thermos of tea. I like my tea strong, almost to the point of bitterness. On location, I can never get anyone to brew it to my taste, and so I do it myself, carry the thermos with me. That's what I offered to her. The thermos of tea I had brewed in my room before going out to the barge.

And did she accept it?

Gratefully. She was shivering. There was quite a sharp wind, the beginning of the mistral, I would imagine. She sat drinking the tea while I explained the scene to her. We were alone in the stern, everyone else was up forward, bustling about, getting ready for the shot.

Did she mention anything about the night before?

24

Not a word. Nor did I expect her to. She only complained that the tea was too bitter. I saw to it that she drank every drop.

Why?

Why? I've already told you. It was uncommonly cold that day. I didn't want to risk her coming down with anything.

Sir . . . was there any other reason for offering her the tea? For making certain that she drank every drop?

What do you mean?

I'm only reiterating now what some of the people on the barge have already said.

Yes, and what's that?

That the girl was drunk when she reported for work, that you tried to sober her up, and that she was still drunk when she went into the water.

Nonsense. No one drinks on my sets. Even if I'd worked with W. C. Fields, I would not have permitted him to drink. And I respected him highly. For an actor, he was a sensitive and decent man.

Yet rumors persist that the girl was drunk when she climbed from the camera barge into the speedboat.

She was cold sober. I would just love to know how such rumors start. The girl finished her tea and was sitting *alone* with me for more than three hours. We were having some color difficulty with the speedboat, I didn't like the way the green bow was registering and I asked that it be repainted. As a result, preparation for the shot took longer than we'd expected. I was afraid it might cloud up and we'd have to move indoors to the cover set. The point is, however, that in all that time not a single soul came anywhere near us. So how in God's name would anyone know whether the girl was drunk or not? Which she wasn't, I can definitely assure you.

They say, sir . . .

25

They, they, who the hell are *they?*

The others on the barge. They say that when she went forward to climb down into the speedboat, she seemed unsure of her footing. They say she appeared glassy-eyed . . .

Rubbish.

. . . that when she asked if the shooting might be postponed . . .

All rubbish.

. . . her voice was weak, somehow without force.

I can tell you definitely and without reservation, and I can tell you as the single human being who was with that girl from the moment she stepped onto the barge until the moment she climbed into the speedboat some three-and-a-half-hours later, that she was at all times alert, responsive, and in complete control of her faculties. She did not want to go into the water because it was cold. But that was a simple fact, and I could not control the temperature of the ocean or the air. Nor could I reasonably postpone shooting when we were in danger of losing our light, and when we finally had everything including the damn speedboat ready to roll.

So she went into the water. As instructed.

Yes. She was supposed to swim a short distance underwater, and then surface. That was the way I'd planned the scene. She went into the water, the cameras were rolling, we . . . none of us quite realized at first that she was taking an uncommonly long time to surface. By the time it dawned upon us, it was too late. *He,* of course, immediately jumped into the water after her . . .

He?

Her leading man, his heroic move, his hairy-chested *star* gesture. She was dead when he reached her.

What caused her to drown? A cramp? Undertow? What?

I haven't the foggiest idea. Accidents happen. What more can I say? This was a particularly unfortunate one, and I regret it. But the past is the past, and if one continues to dwell upon it, one can easily lose sight of the present. I tend not to ruminate. Rumination is only stagnation. I plan ahead and in that way the future never comes as a shock. It's comforting to know, for example, that by the time this appears in print, I will be editing and scoring a film I have not yet begun to shoot. There is verity and substance to routine that varies only slightly. It provides a reality that is all too often lacking in the motion picture industry.

This new film, sir . . .

I thought you'd never ask.

What is it about?

I never discuss the plot or theme of a movie. If I were able to do justice to a story by capsulizing it into three or four paragraphs, why would I then have to spend long months filming it? The synopsis, as such, was invented by Hollywood executives who need so-called 'story analysts' to provide simple translations because they themselves are incapable of reading anything more difficult than "Run, Spot, Run."

What can you tell us about your new film, sir?

I can tell you that it is set in Yugoslavia, and that I will take full cinematic advantage of the rugged coastal terrain there. I can tell you that it is a love story of unsurpassing beauty, and that I have found an unusually talented girl to play the lead. She has never made a film before, she was working with a little theater group on La Cienega when I discovered her, quite by chance. A friend of mine asked me to look in on an original the group was doing, thought there might be film possibilities in it, and so forth. The play was a hopeless botch, but the girl was a revelation. I had her tested immediately, and the results were staggering. What happens before the cameras is all that matters, you know, which is why some of our important stage personalities have never been able to make a successful transition to films. This girl has a vibrancy that causes one to forget completely that there are mechanical appliances such as projectors or screens involved. It is incredible, it is almost uncanny. It is as though her life force transcends the medium itself, sidesteps it so to speak; she achieves direct uninvolved communication at a response level I would never have thought existed. I've been working with her for, oh, easily six months now, and she's remarkably receptive, a rare combination of intelligence and incandescent beauty. I would be foolish to make any sort of prediction about the future, considering the present climate of Hollywood, and the uncertain footing of the entire industry. But if this girl continues to listen and to learn, if she is willing to work as hard in the months ahead as she has already worked, then given the proper vehicle and the proper guidance—both of which I fully intend to supply—I cannot but foresee a brilliant career for her.

Is there anything you would care to say, sir, about the future of the industry in general?

I never deal in generalities, only specifics. I feel that so long as there are men dedicated to the art of making good motion pictures—and I'm not talking now about pornography posing as art, or pathological disorders posing as humor—as long as there are men willing to make the sacrifices necessary to bring quality films to the public, the industry will survive. I intend to survive along with it. In fact, to be more specific, I intend to endure.

Thank you, sir.

The Fallen Angel

He first came in one morning while I was making out the payroll for my small circus. We were pulling up stakes, ready to roll on to the next town, and I was bent over the books, writing down what I was paying everybody, and maybe that is why I did not hear the door open. When I looked up, this long, lanky fellow was standing there, and the door was shut tight behind him.

I looked at the door, and then I looked at him. He had a thin face with a narrow mustache, and black hair on his head that was sort of wild and sticking up in spots. He had brown eyes and a funny, twisted sort of mouth, with very white teeth which he was showing me at the moment.

"Mr. Mullins?" he asked.

"Yes," I said, because that is my name. Not Moon Mullins, which a lot of the fellows jokingly call me, but Anthony Mullins. And that is my real name, with no attempt to sound showman-like; a good name, you will admit. "I am busy," I said.

"I won't take much time," he said very softly. He walked over to the desk with a smooth, sideward step, as if he were on greased ball bearings.

"No matter how much time you will take," I said, "I am still busy."

"My name is Sam Angeli," he said.

"Pleased to meet you, Mr. Angeli," I told him. "My name is Anthony Mullins, and I am sorry you must be running

29

along so quickly, but . . ."

"I'm a trapeze artist," he said.

"We already have three trapeze artists," I informed him, "and they are all excellent performers, and the budget does not call for . . ."

"They are not Sam Angeli," he said, smiling and touching his chest with his thumb.

"That is true," I answered. "They are, in alphabetical order: Sue Ellen Bradley, Edward the Great and Arthur Farnings."

"But not Sam Angeli," he repeated softly.

"No," I said. "It would be difficult to call them all Sam Angeli since they are not even related, and even if they were related, it is unlikely they would all have the same name—even if they were triplets, which they are not."

"*I* am Sam Angeli," he said.

"So I have gathered. But I already have three . . ."

"I'm better," he said flatly.

"I have never met a trapeze artist who was not better than any other trapeze artist in the world," I said.

"In my case it happens to be true," he said.

I nodded and said nothing. I chewed my cigar awhile and went back to my books, and when I looked up he was still standing there, smiling.

"Look, my friend," I said, "I am earnestly sorry there is no opening for you, but . . ."

"Why not watch me a little?"

"I am too busy."

"It'll take five minutes. Your big top is still standing. Just watch me up there for a few minutes, that's all."

"My friend, what would be the point? I already have . . ."

"You can take your books with you, Mr. Mullins; you won't be sorry."

I looked at him again, and he stared at me levelly, and he had a deep, almost blazing, way of staring that made me believe I would really not be sorry if I watched him perform. Besides, I could take the books with me.

"All right," I said, "but we're only wasting each other's time."

"I've got all the time in the world," he answered.

We went outside, and sure enough the big top was still standing, so I bawled out Warren for being so slow to get a show on the road, and then this Angeli and I went inside, and he looked up at the trapeze, and I very sarcastically said, "Is that high enough for you?"

He shrugged and looked up and said, "I've been higher, my friend. Much higher." He dropped his eyes to the ground then, and I saw that the net had already been taken up.

"This exhibition will have to be postponed," I informed him. "There is no net."

"I don't need a net," he answered.

"No?"

"No."

"Do you plan on breaking your neck under one of my tops? I am warning you that my insurance doesn't cover . . ."

"I won't break my neck," Angeli said. "Sit down."

I shrugged and sat down, thinking it was his neck and not mine, and hoping Dr. Lipsky was not drunk as usual. I opened the books on my lap and got to work, and he walked across the tent and started climbing up to the trapeze. I got involved with the figures, and finally he yelled, "Okay, you ready?"

"I'm ready," I said.

I looked up to where he was sitting on one trapeze, holding the bar of the other trapeze in his big hands.

"Here's the idea," he yelled down. He had to yell because

he was a good hundred feet in the air. "I'll set the second trapeze swinging, and then I'll put the one I'm on in motion.
Then I'll jump from one trapeze to the other one. Understand?"

"I understand," I yelled back. I'm a quiet man by nature,
and I have never liked yelling. Besides, he was about to do a
very elementary trapeze routine, so there was nothing to get
excited and yelling about.

He pushed out the second trapeze, and it swung away out
in a nice clean arc, and then it came back and he shoved it out
again and it went out farther and higher this time. He set his
own trapeze in motion then, and both trapezes went swinging
up there, back and forth, back and forth, higher and higher.
He stood up on the bar and watched the second trapeze,
timing himself, and then he shouted down, "I'll do a somersault to make it interesting."

"Go ahead," I said.

"Here I go," he said.

His trapeze came back and started forward, and the
second trapeze reached the end of its arc and started back,
and I saw him bend a little from the knees, calculating his
timing, and then he leaped off, and his head ducked under,
and he went into the somersault.

He did a nice clean roll, and then he stretched out his
hands for the bar of the second trapeze, but the bar was
nowhere near him. His fingers closed on air, and my eyes
popped wide open as he sailed past the trapeze and then
started a nose dive for the ground.

I jumped to my feet with my mouth open, remembering
there was no net under him, and thinking of the mess he was
going to make all over my tent. I watched him falling like a
stone, and then I closed my eyes as he came closer to the
ground. I clenched my fists and waited for the crash, and then

the crash came, and there was a deathly silence in the tent afterward. I sighed and opened my eyes.

Sam Angeli got up and casually brushed the sawdust from his clothes. "How'd you like it?" he asked.

I stood stiff as a board and stared at him.

"How'd you like it?" he repeated.

"Dr. Lipsky!" I shouted. "Doc, come quick!"

"No need for a doctor," Angeli said, smiling and walking over to me. "How'd you like the fall?"

"The . . . the fall?"

"The fall," Angeli said, smiling. "Looked like the real McCoy, didn't it?"

"What do you mean?"

"Well, you don't think I missed that bar accidentally, do you? I mean, after all, that's a kid stunt."

"You fell on purpose?" I kept staring at him, but all his bones seemed to be in the right places, and there was no blood on him anywhere.

"Sure," he said. "My specialty. I figured it all out, Mr. Mullins. Do you know why people like to watch trapeze acts? Not because there's any skill or art attached. Oh, no." He smiled, and his eyes glowed, and I watched him, still amazed. "They like to watch because they are inherently evil, Mr. Mullins. They watch because they think that fool up there is going to fall and break his neck, and they want to be around when he does it." Angeli nodded. "So I figured it all out."

"You did?"

"I did. I figured if the customers wanted to see me fall, then I would fall. So I practiced falling."

"You did?"

"I did. First I fell out of bed, and then I fell from a first-story window, and then I fell off the roof. And then I took my biggest fall, the fall that . . . but I'm boring you. The point is, I

33

can fall from anyplace now. In fact, that trapeze of yours is rather low."

"Rather low," I repeated softly.

"Yes."

"What's up?" Dr. Lipsky shouted, rushing into the tent, his shirttails trailing. "What happened, Moon?"

"Nothing," I said, wagging my head. "Nothing, Doc."

"Then why'd you . . . ?"

"I wanted to tell you," I said slowly, "that I've just hired a new trapeze artist."

"Huh?" Dr. Lipsky said, drunk as usual.

We rolled on to the next town, and I introduced Angeli to my other trapeze artists: Sue Ellen, Farnings, and Edward the Great. I was a younger man at that time, and I have always had an eye for good legs in tights, and Sue Ellen had them all right. She also had blond hair and big blue eyes, and when I introduced her to Angeli those eyes went all over him, and I began to wonder if I hadn't made a mistake hiring him. I told them I wanted Angeli to have exclusive use of the tent that afternoon, and all afternoon I sat and watched him while he jumped for trapezes and missed and went flying down on his nose or his head or his back or whatever he landed on. I kept watching him when he landed, but the sawdust always came up around him like a big cloud, and I never could see what he did inside that cloud. All I know is that he got up every time, and he brushed himself off, and each time I went over to him and expected to find a hundred broken bones and maybe a fractured skull, but each time he just stood up with that handsome smile on his face as if he hadn't just fallen from away up there.

"This is amazing," I told him. "This is almost supernatural!"

34

"I know," he said.

"We'll start you tonight," I said, getting excited about it now. "Can you start tonight?"

"I can start any time," he said.

"Sam Angeli," I announced, spreading my hand across the air as if I were spelling it out in lights. "Sam An—" I paused and let my hand drop. "That's terrible," I said.

"I know," Angeli answered. "But I figured that out, too."

"What?"

"A name for me. I figured this all out."

"And what's the name?" I asked.

"The Fallen Angel," he said.

There wasn't much of a crowd that night. Sue Ellen, Farnings, and Edward the Great went up there and did their routines, but they were playing to cold fish, and you could have put all the applause they got into a sardine can. Except mine. Whenever I saw Sue Ellen, I clapped my heart out, and I never cared what the crowd was doing. I went out after Edward the Great wound up his act, and I said, "Ladeeeees and Gentulmennnn, it gives me great pleasure to introduce at this time, in his American premiere, for the first time in this country, the Fallen Angel!"

I don't know what I expected, but no one so much as batted an eyelid.

"You will note," I said, "that the nets are now being removed from beneath the trapezes, and that the trapezes are being raised to the uppermost portion of the tent. The Fallen Angel will perform at a height of one-hundred-and-fifty-feet above the ground, without benefit of a net, performing his death-defying feats of skill for your satisfaction." The crowd murmured a little, but you could see they still weren't very excited about it all.

"And now," I shouted, "the Fallen Angel!"

Angeli came into the ring, long and thin, muscular in his red tights, the sequins shining so that they could almost blind you. He began climbing up to the bars, and everyone watched him, a little bored by now with all these trapeze acts. Angeli hopped aboard and then worked out a little, swinging to and fro, leaping from one trapeze to another, doing a few difficult stunts. He looked down to the band then, and Charlie started a roll on the drums, and I shouted into my megaphone, "And now, a blood-chilling, spine-tingling double somersault from one moving trapeze to another at one hundred and fifty feet above the ground—*without a net!*"

The crowd leaned forward a little, the way they always will when a snare drum starts rolling, and Angeli set the bars in motion, and then he tensed, with all the spotlights on him. The drum kept going, and then Angeli leaped into space, and he rolled over once, twice, and then his arms came out straight for the bar, and his hands clutched nothing, and he started to fall.

A woman screamed, and then they all were on their feet, a shocked roar leaping from four hundred throats all together. Angeli dropped and dropped and dropped, and women covered their eyes and screamed, and brave men turned away, and then he hit the sawdust, and the cloud rolled up around him, and an *Ohhhhhhh* went up from the crowd. They kept standing, shocked, silent, like a bunch of pallbearers.

Then suddenly, casually, the Fallen Angel got to his feet and brushed off his red-sequined costume. He turned to the crowd and smiled a big, happy smile, and then he turned to face the other half of the tent, smiling again, extending his arms and hands to his public, almost as if he were silently saying, "My children! My nice children!"

The crowd cheered and whistled and shouted and

stamped. Sue Ellen, standing next to me, sighed and said, "Tony, he's wonderful," and I heard her, and I heard the yells of "Encore!" out there, but I didn't bring Angeli out again that night. I tucked him away and then waited for the landslide.

The landslide came the next night. We were playing in a small town, but I think everyone who could walk turned out for the show. They fidgeted through all the acts, crowding the tent, standing in the back, shoving and pushing. They were bored when my aerial artists went on, but the boredom was good because they were all waiting for the Fallen Angel, all waiting to see if the reports about him were true.

When I introduced him, there was no applause. There was only an awful hush. Angeli came out and climbed up to the bars and then began doing his tricks again, and everyone waited, having heard that he took his fall during the double somersault.

But Angeli was a supreme showman, and he realized that the value of his trick lay in its surprise element. So he didn't wait for the double somersault this time. He simply swung out one trapeze and then made a leap for it, right in the middle of his other routine stunts, only this time he missed, and down he dropped with the crowd screaming to its feet.

A lot of people missed the fall, and that was the idea, because those same people came back the next night, and Angeli never did it the same way twice. He'd fall in the middle of his act, or at the end, or once he fell the first time he jumped for the trapeze. Another time he didn't fall at all during the act, and then, as he was coming down the ladder, he missed a rung and down he came, and the crowd screamed.

And Angeli would come to me after each performance and his eyes would glow, and he'd say, "Did you hear them,

Tony? They want me to fall, they want me to break my neck!"

And maybe they did. Or maybe they were just very happy to see him get up after he fell, safe and sound. Whatever it was, it was wonderful. Business was booming, and I began thinking of getting some new tops, and maybe a wild-animal act. I boosted everybody's salary, and I began taking a larger cut myself, and I was finally ready to ask Sue Ellen something I'd wanted to ask her for a long, long time. And Sam Angeli had made it all possible. I spoke to her alone one night, over by the stakes where the elephants were tied.

"Sue Ellen," I said, "there's something that's been on my mind for a long time now."

"What is it, Tony?" she said.

"Well, I'm just a small-time circus man, and I never had much money, you know, and so I never had the right. But things have picked up considerably, and . . ."

"Don't, Tony," she said.

I opened my eyes wide. "I beg your pardon, Sue Ellen?"

"Don't ask me. Maybe it could have been, and maybe it couldn't. But no more now, Tony. Not since I met Sam. He's everything I want, Tony; can you understand that?"

"I suppose," I said.

"I think I love him, Tony."

I nodded and said nothing.

"I'm awfully sorry," Sue Ellen said.

"If it makes you happy, honey . . ."

I couldn't think of any way to finish it.

I started work in earnest. Maybe I should have fired Angeli on the spot, but you can't fire love, and that's what I was battling. So instead I worked harder, and I tried not to see Sue Ellen around all the time. I began to figure crowd reactions, and I realized the people would not hold still for my other aerial artists once they got wind of the Fallen Angel. So we worked Farnings and Edward (whose "Great" title we dropped) into one act, and we worked Sue Ellen into Angeli's act. Sue Ellen dressed up the act a lot, and it gave Angeli someone to kid around with up there, making his stunts before the fall more interesting.

Sue Ellen never did any of the fancy stuff. She just caught Angeli, or was caught by him—all stuff leading up to Angeli's spectacular fall. The beautiful part was that Sue Ellen never had to worry about timing. I mean, if she missed Angeli—so he fell. I thought about his fall a lot, and I tried to figure it out, but I never could, and after a while I stopped figuring. I never stopped thinking about Sue Ellen, though, and it hurt me awful to watch her looking at him with those eyes full of worship, but if she was happy, that was all that counted.

And then I began to get bigger ideas. Why fool around with a small-time circus? I wondered. Why not expand? Why not incorporate?

I got off a few letters to the biggest circuses I knew of. I told them what I had, and I told them the boy was under exclusive contract to me, and I told them he would triple attendance, and I told them I was interested in joining circuses, becoming partners sort of, with the understanding that the Fallen Angel would come along with me. I guess the word had got around by then because all the big-shot letters were very cordial and very nice, and they all asked me when they could get a look at Angeli because they would certainly be interested in incorporating my fine little outfit on a partnership basis if my boy were all I claimed him to be, sincerely yours.

I got off a few more letters, asking all the big shots to attend our regular Friday night performance so that they could judge the crowd reaction and see the Fallen Angel under actual working conditions. All my letters were answered with telegrams, and we set the ball rolling.

That Friday afternoon was pure bedlam.

There's always a million things happening around a circus, anyway, but this Friday everything seemed to pile up at once. Like Fifi, our bareback rider, storming into the tent in her white ruffles.

"My horse!" she yelled, her brown eyes flashing. "My horse!"

"Is something wrong with him?" I asked.

"No, nothing's wrong with him," she screamed. "But something's wrong with José Esperanza, and I'm going to wring his scrawny little neck unless . . ."

"Now easy, honey," I said, "let us take it easy."

"I told him a bucket of *rye*. I did *not* say a bucket of oats. JuJu does not eat oats; he eats rye. And my safety and health and life depend on JuJu, and I will not have him eating some foul-smelling oats when I distinctly told José . . ."

"José!" I bellowed. "José Esperanza, come here."

José was a small Puerto Rican we'd picked up only recently. A nice young kid with big brown cow's eyes and a small timid smile. He poked his head into the wagon and smiled, and then he saw Fifi and the smile dropped from his face.

"Is it true you gave JuJu oats, José, when you were told to give him rye?" I asked.

"*Sí, señor,*" José said, "that ees true."

"But why, José? Why on earth . . ."

José lowered his head. "The horse, *señor*. I like heem. He ees nice horse. He ees always good to me."

"What's that got to do with the bucket of rye?"

"*Señor,*" José said pleadingly, "I did not want to get the horse drunk."

40

"Drunk? Drunk?"

"*Sí, señor*, a bucket of rye. Even for a horse, thees ees a lot of wheesky. I did not theenk . . ."

"Oh," Fifi wailed, "of all the stupid—I'll feed the horse myself. I'll feed him myself. Never mind!"

She stormed out of the wagon, and José smiled sheepishly and said, "I did wrong, *señor?*"

"No," I said. "You did all right, José. Now run along."

I shook my head, and José left, and when I turned around Sam Angeli was standing there. I hadn't heard him come in, and I wondered how long he'd been there, so I said, "A good kid, José."

"If you like good kids," Angeli answered.

"He'll go to heaven, that one," I said. "Mark my words."

Angeli smiled. "We'll see," he said. "I wanted to talk to you, Tony."

"Oh? What about?"

"About all these people coming tonight. The big shots, the ones coming to see me."

"What about them?"

"Nothing, Tony. But suppose—just suppose, mind you—suppose I don't fall?"

"What do you mean?" I said.

"Just that. Suppose I don't fall tonight?"

"That's silly," I said. "You have to fall."

"Do I? Where does it say I have to fall?"

"Your contract. You signed a . . ."

"The contract doesn't say anything about my having to fall, Tony. Not a word."

"Well . . . say, what is this? A holdup?"

"No. Nothing of the sort. I just got to thinking. If this works out tonight, Tony, you're going to be a big man. But what do I get out of it?"

"Do you want a salary boost? Is that it? O.K. You've got a salary boost. How's that?"

"I don't want a salary boost."

"What, then?"

"Something of very little importance. Something of no value whatever."

"What?" I said. "What is it?"

"Suppose we make a deal, Tony?" Angeli said. "Suppose we shake on it? If I fall tonight, I get this little something that I want."

"What's this little something that you want?"

"Is it a deal?"

"I have to know first."

"Well, let's forget it then," Angeli said.

"Now wait a minute, wait a minute. Is this 'thing' Sue Ellen?"

Angeli smiled. "I don't have to make a deal to get her, Tony."

"Well, is it money?"

"No. This thing has no material value."

"Then why do you want it?"

"I collect them."

"And I've got one?"

"Yes."

"Well, what . . . ?"

"Is it a deal, or isn't it?"

"I don't know. I mean, this is a peculiar way to . . ."

"Believe me, this thing is of no material value to you. You won't even know it's gone. But if I go through with my fall tonight, all I ask is that you give it to me. A handshake will be binding as far as I'm concerned."

I shrugged. "All right, all right, a deal. Provided you haven't misrepresented this thing, whatever it is. Provided it's not of material value to me."

"I haven't misrepresented it. Shall we shake, Tony?"

He extended his hand, and I took it, and his eyes glowed, but his skin was very cold to the touch. I pulled my hand away.

"Now," I said, "what's this thing you want from me?"

Angeli smiled. "Your soul," he said.

I was suddenly alone in the wagon. I looked around, but Angeli was gone, and then the door opened and Sue Ellen stepped in, and she looked very grave and very upset.

"I heard," she said. "Forgive me. I heard. I was listening outside. Tony, what are you going to do? What are *we* going to do?"

"Can it be?" I said. "Can it be, Sue Ellen? He looks just like you and me. How'd I get into this?"

"We've got to do something," Sue Ellen said. "Tony, we've got to stop him!"

We packed them in that night. They sat, and they stood, and they climbed all over the rafters; they were everywhere. And right down front, I sat with the big shots, and they all watched my small, unimportant show until it was time for the Fallen Angel to go on.

I got up and smiled weakly and said, "If you gentlemen will excuse me, I have to introduce the next act."

They all smiled back knowingly, and nodded their heads, and their gold stickpins and pinky rings winked at me, and they blew out expensive cigar smoke, and I was thinking, *Mullins, you can blow out expensive cigar smoke, too, but you won't have any soul left.*

I introduced the act, and I was surprised to see all my aerial artists run out onto the sawdust: Sue Ellen, Farnings, Edward and the Fallen Angel. I watched Angeli as he crossed one of the spotlights, and if I'd had any doubts they all vanished right then. Angeli cast no shadow on the sawdust.

I watched in amazement as the entire troupe went up the ladder to the trapezes. There was a smile on Angeli's face, but Sue Ellen and the rest had tight, set mouths.

They did a few stunts, and I watched the big shots, and it was plain they were not impressed at all by these routine aerial acrobatics. I signaled the band, according to schedule, and I shouted, "And now, ladies and gentlemen, the Fallen Angel in a death-defying, spine-tingling, bloodcurdling triple somersault at one hundred and fifty feet above the ground, *without a net!*"

Sue Ellen swung her trapeze out, and Angeli swung his, and then Sue Ellen dropped head downward and extended her hands, and Angeli swung back and forth, and the crowd held its breath, waiting for him to take his fall, and the big shots held their breaths, waiting for the same thing. Only I knew what would happen if he did take that fall. Only I knew about our agreement. Only I—and Sue Ellen, waiting up there for Angeli to jump.

Charlie started the roll on his snare, and then the roll stopped abruptly, and Angeli released his grip on the bar and he swung out into space, and over he went, once, twice, three times—and *slap*. Sue Ellen's hands clamped around his wrists, and she held on for dear life. I couldn't see Angeli's face from so far below, but he seemed to be struggling to get away. Sue Ellen held him for just an instant, just long enough for Edward to swing his trapeze into position.

She flipped Angeli out then, and over he went—and *wham*. Edward grabbed his ankles. Angeli flapped his arms and kicked his legs, trying to get free, but Edward —Edward the Great!—wouldn't drop him. Instead, he swung his trapeze back, and then gave Angeli a flip and

44

Farnings grabbed Angeli's wrists.

Farnings flipped Angeli up, and Sue Ellen caught him, and then Sue Ellen swung her trapeze all the way back and tossed Angeli to Edward, and I began to get the idea of what was going on up there.

Edward tossed Angeli, and Farnings caught him, and then Farnings tossed him to Sue Ellen, and Sue Ellen tossed him right back again. Then Farnings climbed onto Sue Ellen's trapeze, and they both swung back to the platform.

Edward took a long swing, and then he tossed Angeli head over heels, right back to the platform, where Sue Ellen and Farnings grabbed him with four eager arms.

I was grinning all over by this time, and the crowd was booing at the top of its lungs. Who cared? The big shots were stirring restlessly, but they'd probably heard that Angeli sometimes fell coming down the ladder, and so they didn't leave their seats.

Only tonight, Angeli wasn't doing any falling coming down any ladder. Because Sue Ellen had one of his wrists and Farnings had one of his ankles, and one was behind him, and the other was ahead of him; and even if he pitched himself off into space, he wouldn't have gone far, not with the grips they had on both him and the ladder. I saw the big shots get up and throw away their cigars, and then everybody began booing as if they wanted to tear down the top with their voices. Angeli came over to me, and his face didn't hold a pleasant smile this time. His face was in rage, and it turned red, as if he would explode.

"You tricked me!" he screamed. "You tricked me!"

"Oh, go to hell," I told him, and all at once he wasn't there any more.

Well, I'm not John Ringling North, and I don't run the

greatest show on earth. I've just got a small, unimportant circus, and it gives me a regular small income, but it's also a lot of trouble sometimes.

I still have my soul, though; and, what's more, I now have a soulmate, and she answers to the name of Sue Ellen Mullins, which is in a way most euphonic, you will agree.

The Prisoner

They were telling the same tired jokes in the squadroom when Randolph came in with his prisoner.

Outside the grilled windows, October lay like a copper coin, and the sun struck only glancing blows at the pavement. The season had changed, but the jokes had not, and the climate inside the squadroom was one of stale cigarette smoke and male perspiration. For a tired moment, Randolph had the feeling that the room was suspended in time, unchanging, unmoving and that he would see the same faces and hear the same jokes until he was an old, old man.

He had led the girl up the precinct steps, past the hanging green globes, past the desk in the entrance corridor, nodding perfunctorily at the desk sergeant. He had walked beneath the white sign with its black-lettered DETECTIVE DIVISION and its pointing hand, and then had climbed the steps to the second floor of the building, never once looking back at the girl, knowing that in her terror and uncertainty she was following him. When he reached the slatted rail divider that separated the corridor from the detective squadroom, he heard Burroughs telling his old joke, and perhaps it was the joke that caused him to turn harshly to the girl.

"Sit down," he said. "On that bench!"

The girl winced at the sound of his voice. She was a thin girl wearing a straight skirt and a faded green cardigan. Her hair was a bleached blonde, the roots growing in brown. She had wide blue eyes, and they served as the focal point of an otherwise uninteresting face. She had slashed lipstick across her mouth in a wide, garish red smear. She flinched when Randolph spoke, and then she backed away from him and went to sit on the wooden bench in the corridor, opposite the men's room.

Randolph glanced at her briefly, the way he would look at a bulletin board notice about the Policeman's Ball. Then he pushed through the rail divider and walked directly to Burroughs' desk.

"Any calls?" he asked.

"Oh, hi, Frank," Burroughs said. "No calls. You're interrupting a joke."

"I'm sure it's hilarious."

"Well, I think it's pretty funny," Burroughs said defensively.

"I thought it was pretty funny, too," Randolph said, "the first hundred times."

He stood over Burroughs' desk, a tall man with close-cropped brown hair and lusterless brown eyes. His nose had been broken once in a street fight, and together with the hard, unyielding line of his mouth, it gave his face an over-all look of meanness. He knew he was intimidating Burroughs, but he didn't much give a damn. He almost wished that Burroughs would really take offense and come out of the chair fighting. There was nothing he'd have liked better than to knock Burroughs on his ass.

"You don't like the jokes, you don't have to listen," Burroughs said, but his voice lacked conviction.

"Thank you. I won't."

From a typewriter at the next desk Dave Fields looked up. Fields was a big cop with shrewd blue eyes and a friendly smile. The smile belied the fact that he could be the toughest cop in the precinct when he wanted to.

"What's eating you, Frank?" he asked, smiling.

"Nothing. What's eating you?"

Fields continued smiling. "You looking for a fight?" he asked.

Randolph studied him. He had seen Fields in action, and he was not particularly anxious to provoke him. He wanted to smile back and say something like, "Ah, the hell with it. I'm just down in the dumps"—anything to let Fields know he had no real quarrel with him. But something else inside him took over, something that had not been a part of him long ago.

He held Fields' eyes with his own. "Anytime you're ready for one," he said, and there was no smile on his mouth.

"He's got the crud," Fields said. "Every month or so, the bulls in this precinct get the crud. It's from dealing with criminal types."

He recognized Fields' maneuver and was grateful for it. Fields was smoothing it over. Fields didn't want trouble, and so he was joking his way out of it now, handling it as it should have been handled. But whereas he realized Fields was being the bigger of the two men, he was still immensely satisfied that he had not backed down. Yet his satisfaction rankled.

"I'll give you some advice," Fields said. "You want some advice, Frank? Free?"

"Go ahead," Randolph said.

"Don't let it get you. The trouble with being a cop in a precinct like this one is that you begin to imagine everybody in the world is crooked. That just ain't so."

"No, huh?"

"Believe me, Frank, it ain't."

"Thanks," Randolph said. "I've been a cop in this precinct for eight years now. I don't need advice on how to be a cop in this precinct."

"All right, get in there!" a voice in the corridor shouted.

Randolph turned. He saw Boglio first, and then he saw the man with Boglio. The man was small and thin with a narrow mustache. He had brown eyes and lank brown hair, and he wet his mustache nervously with his tongue.

"Over there!" Boglio shouted. "Against the wall!"

"What've you got, Rudy?" Randolph asked.

"I got a punk," Boglio said. He turned to the man and bellowed, "You hear me? Get the hell over against that wall!"

"What'd he do?" Fields asked.

Boglio didn't answer. He shoved out at the man, slamming him against the wall alongside the filing cabinets. "What's your name?" he shouted.

"Arthur," the man said.

"Arthur *what?*"

"Arthur Semmers."

"You drunk, Semmers?"

"No."

"Are you high?"

"What?"

"Are you on junk?"

"What's—I don't understand what you mean."

"Narcotics. Answer me, Semmers."

"Narcotics? Me? No, I ain't never touched it, I swear."

"I'm gonna ask you some questions, Semmers," Boglio said. "You want to get this, Frank?"

"I've got a prisoner outside," Randolph said.

"The little girl on the bench?" Boglio asked. His eyes locked with Randolph's for a moment. "That can wait. This is business."

"Okay," Randolph said. He took a pad from his back pocket and sat in a straight-backed chair near where Semmers stood crouched against the wall.

50

"Name's Arthur Semmers," Boglio said. "You got that, Frank?"

"Spell it," Randolph said.

"S-E-M-M-E-R-S," Semmers said.

"How old are you, Semmers?" Boglio asked.

"Thirty-one."

"Born in this country?"

"Sure. Hey, what do you take me for, a greenhorn? Sure, I was born right here."

"Where do you live?"

"Eighteen-twelve South Fourth."

"You getting this, Frank?"

"I'm getting it," Randolph said.

"All right, Semmers, tell me about it."

"What do you want to know?"

"I want to know why you cut up that kid."

"I didn't cut up nobody."

"Semmers, let's get something straight. You're in a squadroom now, you dig me? You ain't out in the street where we play the game by your rules. This is *my* ball park, Semmers. You don't play the game my way, and you're gonna wind up with the bat I rammed down your throat."

"I still didn't cut up nobody."

"Okay, Semmers," Boglio said. "Let's start it this way. Were you on Ashley Avenue, or weren't you?"

"Sure, I was. There's a law against it?"

"Were you anywhere near 467 Ashley?"

"Yeah."

"Semmers, there was a man stabbed in front of 467 Ashley. He was stabbed four times, and we already took him to the hospital, and he's liable to die. You know what homicide is, Semmers?"

"That's when somebody gets killed."

"You know what Homicide cops are like?"

"No. What?"

"You'd be laying on the floor almost dead by now if you was up at Homicide. Just thank God you're here, Semmers, and don't try my patience."

"I never seen the guy. I never cut up nobody."

Without warning, Boglio drew back his fist and smashed it into Semmers' face. Semmers lurched back against the wall, bounced off it like a handball, and then clasped his shattered lip with his hand.

"Why'd you—"

"Shut up!" Boglio yelled.

From where he sat, Randolph could see the blood spurting from Semmers' mouth. Dispassionately, he watched.

"Tell me about the stabbing," Boglio said.

"There ain't nothing to—"

Again, Boglio hit him, harder this time.

"Tell me about the stabbing," he repeated.

"I . . ."

The fist lashed out again. Randolph watched.

"You going to need me any more?" he asked Boglio.

"No," Boglio said, drawing back his fist.

From across the room, Fields said, "For Christ's sake, lay off, Rudy. You want to kill the poor bastard?"

"I don't like punks," Boglio said. He turned again to the bloody figure against the wall.

Randolph rose, ripped the pages of notes from the black book, and put them on Boglio's desk. He was going through the gate in the railing when Fields stopped him.

"How does it feel?" Fields asked.

"What do you mean?"

"Being an accomplice."

"I don't know what you're talking about," Randolph said.

"Don't you?"

"No."

"You beginning to think the way Boglio does? About punks, I mean?"

"My thoughts are my business, Dave," Randolph said. "Keep out of them."

"Boglio's thoughts are his business, too."

"He's questioning a punk who knifed somebody. What the hell do you want him to do?"

"He's questioning a human being who maybe *did* and maybe *didn't* knife somebody."

"What's the matter, Dave? You in love with this precinct?"

"I think it stinks," Fields said. "I think it's a big, stinking prison."

"All right. So do I!"

"But for Christ's sake, Frank, learn who the prisoners are! Don't become—"

"I can take care of myself," Randolph said.

Fields sighed. "What are your plans for the little girl outside?"

"She's trash," Randolph said.

"So?"

"So what do you want? Go back to the D.D. report you were typing, Dave. I'll handle my own prisoners."

"Sure," Fields said, and turned and walked to his desk.

Randolph watched his retreating back. Casually, he lighted a cigarette and then walked out into the corridor. The girl looked up as he approached. Her eyes looked very blue in the dimness of the corridor. Very blue and very frightened.

"What's your name?" Randolph asked.

"Betty," the girl said.

"You're in trouble, Betty," Randolph said flatly.

"I . . . I know."

"How old are you, Betty?"

"Twenty-four."

"You look younger."

The girl hesitated. "That's . . . that's because I'm so skinny," she said.

"You're not that skinny," Randolph said harshly. "Don't play the poor little slum kid with me."

"I wasn't playing anything," Betty said. "I *am* skinny. I know I am. It's nothing to be ashamed of."

Her voice was very soft, the voice of a young girl, a frightened young girl. He looked at her, and he told himself, *She's a tramp,* and his mind clicked shut like a trap.

"Lots of girls are skinny," Betty said. "I know lots of girls who—"

"Let's lay off the skinny routine," Randolph said dryly. "We already made that point." He paused. "You're twenty-four, huh?"

"Yes." She nodded and a quiet smile formed on her painted mouth. "How old are you?"

"I'm thirty-two," Randolph said before he could catch himself, and then he dropped his cigarette angrily to the floor and stepped on it. "You mind if I ask the questions?"

"I was only curious. You seem . . . never mind."

"What do I seem?"

"Nothing."

"All right, let's get down to business. How long have you been a hooker?"

The girl looked at him blankly. "What?"

"Don't you hear good?"

"Yes, but what does hooker mean?"

Randolph sighed heavily. "Honey," he said, "the sooner

we drop the wide-eyed innocence, the better off we'll both be."

"But I don't—"

"A hooker is a prostitute!" Randolph said, his voice rising. "Now come off it!"

"Oh," the girl said.

"Oh," Randolph repeated sarcastically. "Now how long?"

"This . . . this was my first time."

"Sure."

"Really," she said eagerly. "I'd . . . I'd never gone out looking for . . . for men before. This was my first time."

"And you picked me, huh?" Randolph asked, unbelievingly. "Well, honey, you picked the wrong man for your first one."

"I didn't know you were a cop."

"Now you know."

"Yes. Now I know."

"And you also know you're in pretty big trouble."

"Yes," the girl said.

"Good," Randolph answered, grinning.

Actually, the girl wasn't in as much trouble as she imagined herself to be—and Randolph knew it. She had indeed stopped him on the street and asked, "Want some fun, mister?" and Randolph had immediately put the collar on her. But in the city for which Randolph worked, it would have been next to impossible to make a prostitution charge stick. Randolph conceivably had a "dis cond" case, but disorderly conduct was a dime-a-dozen misdemeanor and was hardly worth bothering with in a precinct where felonies ran wild. So Randolph knew all this, and he had known it when he collared the girl, and he sat now with a grin on his face and watched her, pleased by her troubled expression, pleased with the way her hands fluttered aimlessly in her lap.

"You can get out of it," he said softly.

"How?" the girl asked eagerly.

His voice dropped to a whisper. "If you know the right cop," he said.

The girl stared at him blankly for a moment. "I haven't any money," she said at last. "I . . . I wouldn't have done this if I had money."

"There are other ways," Randolph said.

"Oh." She stared at him and then nodded slightly. "I see."

"Well?"

"Yes," she said, still nodding. "All right. Whatever you say."

"Let's go," Randolph said.

He walked briskly to the railing and leaned on it. To no one in particular, he said, "I'll be back in an hour or so." Before he turned, he noticed the curiously sour expression on Dave Fields' face. Briskly, he walked to the girl. "Come on," he said.

They went down the steps to the ground floor. At the desk, a patrolman was booking a seventeen-year-old kid who was bleeding from a large cut behind his ear. The blood had trailed down his neck and stained his tee-shirt a bright red. The girl gasped when she saw the boy, and then turned quickly away, heading for the steps.

"If he's the one they're booking," Randolph said, "I hate to think what the other guy must took like."

The girl didn't answer. She began walking quickly, and Randolph fell in beside her. "Where to?" he asked.

"My house," she said. An undisguised coldness had crept into her voice.

"Don't take this so big," he said. "It's part of a working day."

"I didn't know that," the girl said.

"Well, now you do."

They walked in silence. Around them, the concrete fingers of the city poked at the October sky. The fingers were black with the soot of decades, grimy fingers covered with waste and not with the honest dirt of labor. The streets crawled with humanity. Old men and young men, kids playing stickball, kids chalking up the sidewalks, women with shopping bags, the honest citizens of the precinct—and the others. In the ten minutes it took them to walk from the precinct to the girl's apartment, Randolph saw fourteen junkies in the streets. Some of those junkies would be mugging before the day ended. Some would be shoplifting and committing bur-glaries. All would be blind by nightfall.

He saw the bright green-and-yellow silk jackets of a teenage gang known as "The Marauders," and he knew that the appearance of a blue-and-gold jacket in their territory would bring on a street bop and broken ribs and bloody heads.

He saw the hookers and the pimps and the sneak thieves and the muggers and the ex-cons and the kids holding JD cards and the drunks and the fences and the peddlers of hot goods—he saw them all, and they surrounded him with a feeling of filth, a feeling he wanted desperately to search out and crush because somewhere in the filth he had lost himself.

Somewhere, long ago, a young patrolman had cracked a liquor store holdup, and the patrolman had been promoted to detective third grade, and the patrolman's name was Frank Randolph. And somewhere back there the patrolman Frank Randolph had ceased to exist and the detective Frank Randolph had inhabited the shell of his body. The eyes had turned hard, and the fists had turned quick, and the step had turned cautious because there was danger in these streets, and the danger awakened every animal instinct within a man, reduced him to a beast stalking blood in the narrow, dark passages of the jungle.

There was hatred within the muscular body of Frank Randolph, a hatred bred of dealing with tigers, a hatred that excluded the timid antelopes who also lived in the forest.

And so he walked with a young, thin girl, walked toward her apartment where he would use his shield as a wedge to enter her bed and her body. He had begun using his shield a long time ago. He was as much an addict to his shield as the junkies in the streets were addicts to the white god.

The tenement stood in a row of somber-faced buildings, buildings that solemnly mourned the loss of their latter-day splendor. The fire escapes fronting each building were hung with the trappings of life: blankets, potted plants, pillows, empty beer cans, ash trays, guitars. Autumn had come late this year, lingering over the slow death of a hot summer, and the cliff dwellers had taken to their slum terraces, the iron-barred rectangles that gave them a piece of sky and a breath of air.

"This is it," she said.

He followed her up the stoop. A woman was sitting on the steps, knitting. She glanced up at him as he passed, sensing immediately, with the instinct of self-preservation, that he was a cop. He could almost feel her shrinking away from him, and his own instinct asked the question, "What's she done to be afraid of?"

Garbage cans were stacked in the hallway. The refuse had been collected earlier that day, but the cans were never washed and they filled the air with the stink of waste. There was a naked light bulb hanging in the entrance foyer, but it would not be turned on until dusk.

The girl climbed the steps ahead of him. He walked

behind her; her legs were remarkably good for a girl so thin. They climbed steadily. There were voices behind the doors. He heard the voices in the medley of sound, and he reflected on the doors he had broken, a quick flat-footed kick against the lock to spring it, since he'd been a detective. Rarely had he knocked on a door. Rarely had he given the occupant a chance to unlatch it. The kick was quicker, and it precluded the possibility of a door being opened to reveal a hostile gun inside.

"It's on the third floor," the girl said.

"All right," he answered, and he kept following her, watching her legs.

"Be careful, there's a broken bottle."

He skirted the shards of brown glass, smelling the whiskey fumes as he passed the alcohol-soaked wood. The girl stopped at a door at the end of the hall. She unlocked it and waited for him to enter. When they were both inside, she put the police lock in place, leaning the heavy, unbending steel bar against the door, hooking it securely into the steel plate embedded in the floor, so that it formed a formidable triangle against which entrance was impossible.

The kitchen was small but clean. A round table sat in the center of the room, and a bowl was on the table. A single apple rested in the bowl. The girl went to the window and lifted the shade. Light, but not sunlight, entered the room. It was a pale light that bounced from the brick walls of the tenement not four feet away, leaping the airshaft between the buildings. The girl turned.

"I . . . I don't know what to do," she said. "I've never done this before."

"No?" he said, and there was a trace of sarcasm in his voice.

"No. Could . . . could we talk a little?"

"What about?"

"I don't know. Anything." The room grew silent. Patiently, Randolph waited.

"I'm . . . I'm sorry the place isn't nicer," the girl said.

"It'll do."

"I meant—" She shrugged.

"What?"

"I don't know. A girl likes to think—" She stopped, shrugging again. "Would you like a beer or something? I think we have some cold in the refrigerator."

"No, thanks," Randolph said. He grinned. "We're not allowed to drink on duty."

The girl missed his humor. She nodded and then sat opposite him at the table. Silence crowded the room again.

"Have you been a cop long?" the girl asked.

"Eight years."

"It must be terrible. I mean, being a cop in this neighborhood."

For a moment, Randolph was surprised. He looked at the girl curiously and said, "What do you mean?"

"All the . . . all the dirt here," she said.

"It . . ." He paused, studying her. "You get used to it."

"I'll never get used to it," she said.

She seemed about to cry. For a panicky instant, he wanted to bolt from the room. He sat, undecided, at the table, and then he heard himself saying, "This isn't so bad. This is a nice apartment."

"You don't really mean that," she said.

"No," he answered honestly. "I don't."

The girl seemed to want to tell him about the apartment. Words were perched on the edge of her tongue, torrents of words, it seemed, but when she spoke she only said, "I haven't got my own room."

"That's all right," he said. "We can use . . ." And then he

stopped his tongue because he sensed the girl had not wanted to say that at all, and the sudden insight surprised him and frightened him a little.

"Where do you live?" she asked.

"In a hotel," he said.

"That must be nice."

He wanted to say, "No, it's very lonely." Instead, he said, "Yeah, it's all right."

"I've never been to a hotel. Do people wait on you?"

"This is an apartment hotel. It's a little different."

"Oh."

She sat at the table, and he watched her, and suddenly she was trembling.

"What's the matter?" he asked.

"I'm scared," she said.

"Why?"

"Because of . . . of what I almost did. What I almost became."

"What do you mean?"

"I'm glad you arrested me," she said. "I'm glad I got caught the first time. I don't want to be . . ."

She began crying. Randolph watched her, and he felt inordinately big, sitting across from her, awkwardly immense.

"Look," he said, "what do you want to bawl for?"

"I . . . I can't help it."

"Well, cut it out!" he said harshly.

"I'm sorry." She turned and took a dishtowel from the sink, daubed at her eyes with it. "I'm sorry. Let's . . . let's do it."

"Is this really your first time?" he asked suspiciously.

"Yes."

"What made you . . . well . . . I don't understand."

"I got tired," she said. "I got so damned tired. I don't

want to fight any more."

"Fight what?"

"Fight getting dirty. I'm tired of fighting." She sighed wearily and held out her hand. "Come," she said.

She stood stock still, her hand extended, her shoulders back.

"Come," she repeated.

There was a strength in the rigidity of her body and the erectness of her head. In the narrow stillness of her thin body, there was a strength, and he recognized the strength because he had once possessed it. He rose, puzzled, and he reached out for her hand, and he knew that if he took her hand, if he allowed this girl to lead him into the other room, he would destroy her as surely as he had once destroyed himself. He knew this, and somehow it was very important to him that she be saved, that somewhere in the prison of the precinct, somewhere in this giant, dim, dank prison there should be someone who was not a prisoner. And he knew with sudden painful clarity why there were potted plants on the barred fire escapes of the tenements.

He pulled back his hand.

"Keep it," he said harshly, swiftly.

"What?"

"Keep it," he said, and he knew she misunderstood what he was asking her to keep, but he did not explain. He turned and walked from the room, and down the steps past the stacked garbage cans in the hallway and then out into the street.

He walked briskly in the afternoon sunshine. He saw the pushers and the pimps and the prostitutes and the junkies and the fences and the drunks and the muggers.

And when he got back to the station house, he nodded perfunctorily at the desk sergeant and then climbed the stairs to the Detective Division.

Dave Fields met him just inside the slatted rail divider. Their eyes met, locked.

"How'd you make out?" Fields asked.

Unwaveringly, unhesitatingly, Randolph replied, "Fine. The best fuck I've ever had," and Fields turned away when he saw the smirk on his face.

Terminal Misunderstanding

The man on the other end of the wire was somewhat intoxicated. I kept telling him I was calling from Chicago and that I wanted to speak to my wife, Abby Eisler. I spelled her name three times for him.

"You should see the crowd here," he said. "This's a real nice crowd here."

"Yes, I can hear it," I said. "Would you please . . . ?"

"This's a real nice party," he said. "Who's this calling?"

"Sam Eisler," I said. "I want to talk to my wife, Abby."

"Sam, whyn't you come on up here?" he said. "This's a real nice party."

"I'm *supposed* to come up there," I said, "that's just it. I'm in Chicago. My plane put down . . ." I hesitated and then looked at the telephone receiver as if it had somehow beguiled me into detailing my predicament to a drunk. "Look," I said, "would you please yell out my wife's name and tell her she's wanted on the telephone?"

"Sure," he said. "What's your wife's name?"

"Abby Eisler."

"Who's this calling?"

"Sam Eisler. Her husband."

"Sure, Sam, wait just one minute."

I waited. I heard the small plastic rattle of the receiver as he put it down, and then I heard him bellowing, "Annie Iceman! Telephone! Annie Iceman wanted on the telephone," his voice receding as he went further and further

64

away from the instrument, until finally it was drowned out by all the party noises. Wonderful, I thought. He's wandered away and left the phone off the hook. Now I'll *never* get through to her. I kept waiting.

"Hello?" a voice said at last. It was Abby.

"Is this Annie Iceman?" I said.

"Sam!" she said immediately. "Are you back?"

"Not quite."

"What do you mean not quite? How can you be not *quite* back?"

"I can be in Chicago," I said. "At O'Hare. The whole eastern seaboard's socked in. They put us down here in Chicago."

"How can they do that? You bought a ticket for New York, didn't you?"

"Yes, of course I . . . Abby, are *you* drunk, too? Is everybody at that goddamn party drunk already?"

"Of course I'm certainly not drunk," Abby said. "How long is it from Chicago?"

"How long is *what*, Abby?"

"The train ride, naturally."

"I don't know. Overnight, I would guess. Anyway, I'm not about to take a train."

"Randy, would you please fill this for me, please?" Abby said.

"Who's Randy?"

"He's the head of creation someplace."

"Only *God* is the head of creation," I said.

"Well, somebody said Randy is, too. I was just now sitting out on the fire escape with him when you called."

"Since when do you go sitting on fire escapes with strange men?"

"He's not strange, he's very nice."

65

"Nice or otherwise, since when . . ."

"Since about nine-thirty, I guess. What time is it now?"

"In New York or in Chicago?"

"Anyplace," Abby said. "Oh thank you, Randy."

"How many of those have you had?" I said.

"Which?"

"Whatever you're drinking there."

"Oh, two or three, I guess. Listen, why'd you ask for Annie Iceman? That's not very funny."

"I *didn't* ask for Annie Iceman. The guy who answered the phone was loaded."

"It's just not very *funny*," Abby said. "Sam, when do you think you'll get here?"

"I don't know. I'm going to check in at the information desk as soon as I hang up, see if there's a chance of the fog lifting tonight. If not, I guess I'll have to sleep over."

"What should *I* do?"

"I would suggest that you come in off the fire escape. A thirty-eight-year-old lady shouldn't be sitting on the fire escape in a fog."

"Sam, you *don't* have to keep reminding me I'm thirty-eight. *I* don't keep reminding *you* you're forty-one."

"Well, *I'm* not out on the fire escape."

"Neither am I," Abby said. "What should I tell John and Louise?"

"Tell them I'm stuck in Chicago and may have to skip their party."

"Well, okay," Abby said, and sighed.

"Abby?"

"Mmm?"

"I miss you."

"I miss you, too," she said.

"Goddamn airline," I said.

"Mmm," she said. "Sam?"

"Yes, honey?"

"I *still* don't think asking for Annie Iceman was very funny," she said, and hung up.

The operator, who had *not* signaled to tell me when I was talking overtime (as I'd asked her to do), now told me that I owed the telephone company a dollar and forty cents. I walked over to the cigar stand, changed a five-dollar bill, and then went back to the telephone to deposit the overtime money. I picked up my two-suiter at the baggage claim counter, and then walked through the terminal to the information desk. The airline's ground hostess informed me that the forecast for Kennedy was still fog until morning, but that all Los Angeles-New York passengers were being provided with either rail transportation to New York or, if they preferred, overnight hotel accommodations in Chicago.

"Why didn't the airline *tell* us that New York was fogged in?" I said.

"Didn't the pilot make an announcement, sir?"

"Why didn't they tell us in Los Angeles? *Before* we took off."

"I'm sorry, sir," she said, "I don't have that information."

"I mean, I don't know how long it takes to transmit a weather report across the nation, but New York is three hours *ahead* of Los Angeles, and it seems to me that unless this fog just suddenly materialized out of thin air and *pounced* down on Kennedy, it seems to me somebody in your wide-awake little outfit should have informed the passengers while we were still on the ground in Los Angeles. So that we could have decided for ourselves whether we wanted to spend the night *there* or here in Chicago. I don't know about you, Miss, but Chicago has never been one of my favorite sleeping cities."

"Well, sir," she said, "I don't control the weather in New York."

"Where *do* you control the weather?" I asked.

"Sir?" she said.

"There's a man in New York your airline ought to hire. His name is Randy, he's the head of creation."

"Sir?"

"How do you expect to get that million-dollar bonus if you treat your passengers this way?"

"You're thinking of another airline," she said, and then turned away curtly to assist a sailor who looked as though he had never been outside of Iowa in his life and was now totally bewildered by jet terminals and smiling hostesses and glowering New York attorneys like *me*, Samuel Eisler. I kept glaring at the girl's back until I was sure my indignation had burned clear through to her spine, and then I stalked off angrily in the direction of the airport bar.

Jennifer Logan was making a phone call in an open booth not a hundred yards from the information desk. She was wearing a very short green mini, a dark-green cashmere cardigan, and sandals. Her long blond hair spilled over the receiver as she spoke, and she brushed it away from her face impatiently and then said into the phone, "Well, you know, Marcie, what would you *like* me to do? Hijack a damn airplane? I'm telling you I can't get *on*. Yes, *sure*, I'm wait-listed, but that can mean tonight or tomorrow or maybe St. Swithin's Day." Jennifer paused, pulled a face, looked directly at me, smiled, waggled the fingers on her free hand, whispered, "Hi, Mr. Eisler," and then said into the phone, "St. *Swithin's*. Oh never mind, Marcie." She paused again, and then said, "When I *get* there. I'll *get* there. Meanwhile, I see somebody I know. Give my love to Paul." She hung up, felt in the return chute for any unexpected bonanza, rose, left her two suitcases and what appeared to be a hatbox outside the booth, reslung her shoulder bag, and walked toward me with her hand extended.

"Hi, Mr. Eisler," she said again.

"Hello, Jennifer," I said. "How are you?"

"Exhausted," she said, and rolled her eyes. "I can't get on a damn plane to San Francisco. I mean, I probably *could* get on a plane if I wanted to pay the regular fare, but I'm holding out for the student rate, and there're like seven million kids trying to get back at the same time. It's murder."

"Are you going to school in San Francisco now?" I asked.

"Mmm, Berkeley," she said. "What are you doing in Chicago, Mr. Eisler?"

"I'm in transit. New York's fogged in."

"Oh," Jennifer said. "Hey, I'll bet *that's* what's causing the pile-up here, don't you think?"

"Maybe."

"I've never *seen* so many kids in my entire life," she said. "So you're stuck here, huh?"

"Looks that way."

"What're you going to do?"

"Right now, I'm going to get a drink."

"Good idea," she said. "Let me get my bags."

I watched her in surprise as she walked toward her luggage. I would not have asked Jennifer Logan to join me for a drink three years ago, and I honestly had not intended my flat statement of purpose as an invitation now. But she picked up one suitcase, and then the hatbox, and then looked up plaintively and said, "Mr. Eisler, could you give me a hand with this?" and I found myself walking to her swiftly and picking up the second suitcase and then carrying that and my own two-suiter through the terminal while she walked swiftly beside me chattering about her habit of always carrying too

much crap with her, like the wig, now *really* she didn't need to
take the wig home for spring vacation, did she? None of the
other kids . . .

"Is that a wig?" I asked.

"Yes, a short one. It's all curls like."

"I thought it was a hat."

"No, it's a wig."

. . . traveled with as much luggage as she did. She always
came into an airport looking like a Russian peasant lady or
something, it was really quite disgraceful.

"You don't look at all like a Russian peasant lady," I
said.

"What *do* I look like?" she asked, and then smiled quickly
and ducked her head, long blond strands falling over her
cheek, hand holding the wig box brushing them back again,
and added, "Never mind, don't tell me."

I was a little out of breath. She was walking with swift
long-legged strides, her sandals slapping along beside me,
spewing her rapid monologue, telling me she shouldn't have
come all the way east to begin with, and *wouldn't* have come if
her parents hadn't offered a sort of a bribe . . .

"How *are* your parents?" I asked.

"Oh, fine," she said.

. . . agreeing to take her down to Nassau with them for the
Spring break, though you'd never guess she'd been South,
the sun hadn't come out the whole week she'd been there.
She'd expected to go back to San Francisco with at least *some*
kind of a tan, and instead she looked like a sickly white thing
that had crawled out from under a rock.

"You look very healthy, Jennifer," I said.

"Depends where you're looking," she answered, and
flashed her quick grin again, and before I had time to think
about what she'd just said, she stopped before what was

undoubtedly the airport bar and said, "Is this it?"

"I guess so."

"Let me get the door," she said, and reached out with the hand still clutching the wig box. After a lot of awkward shuffling and maneuvering, we finally managed to squeeze the three suitcases, the wig box and ourselves through the door and over to the checkroom, where I deposited the luggage with an enormous sense of relief.

"*Made* it!" Jennifer said triumphantly.

"I wasn't sure we would."

"Neither was I."

"What do you mean?"

"The way you were puffing back there. I see a table, come on."

The bar was fairly crowded and resounding with the same kind of noise I had heard over the telephone wires from New York. Jennifer led me to an unoccupied table against the rear wall, and we slid in behind it on the leatherette banquette. I immediately signaled to the waiter.

"Seat's warm," Jennifer said. "Must have been a very fat lady sitting here."

The waiter, a crew-cut, clean-shaved kid who looked to be twenty-two or -three ambled over, stared admiringly at Jennifer, glanced balefully at me, and then said, "Yes, sir, can I help you?"

"Jennifer?"

"I'd like a scotch on the rocks, please," she said.

"A scotch for the lady," I said, "and I'll have . . ."

"Excuse me, Miss," the waiter said, "but would you happen to have some identification with you?"

"Flatterer," Jennifer said, and immediately unslung her shoulder bag, opened it, and produced her ID card. The waiter studied it as though I were a white slaver transporting nubile blondes across state lines. As his scrutiny persisted, I felt first embarrassment, and then anger.

"The young lady's over twenty-one," I snapped. "If you're finished with her card, we'd like some drinks here."

"Sorry, sir," the waiter said, "but I don't make the laws in this state."

"Do you control the weather here?"

"Huh?"

"Just give the young lady her card, and bring us a scotch on the rocks and a vodka martini, straight up."

"We could lose our license, you know," the waiter said.

"*We* could lose our *patience*," I said, and gave him the same penetrating, disintegrating look I had wasted on the hostess' back.

The waiter dropped Jennifer's card on the table top, mumbled, "Scotch on the rocks, vodka martini, straight up," and then walked off with a cowpuncher's lope.

"My, my," Jennifer said, picking up her card and putting it back in her bag, "you *do* take control of a situation, don't you?"

"I get vicious when I'm thirsty."

"What it probably was," Jennifer said, "is that he probably figures you're too old for me."

"Well, yes," I said, "but still, you know, you did, you know, show him the identification he asked for, you know, and he had no right . . ."

"Don't get nervous," Jennifer said. "I'm not coming on or anything."

"I'm not nervous," I said.

"You seem nervous."

"I'm not."

"Okay. Do you always drink martinis?"

"Not always."

"I mean, this late at night. I thought people only drank martinis before dinner."

"I haven't *had* dinner yet," I said.

"Didn't you eat on the plane?"

"Yes, but that would hardly qualify as dinner."

"I never eat on airplanes, either," she said. "I get like a ravenous beast, but I'll be damned if I'll eat any of that plastic crap they serve. I'm starved right now, to tell the truth, I haven't eaten since early this morning. What I did, you see, was grab a plane from New York because I couldn't get a San Francisco flight, and I figured Chicago's better than nothing, don't you think? Closer to where I'm headed, anyway."

"Wasn't it foggy?"

"Where?"

"In New York."

"No. Not when I left."

"Scotch on the rocks." the waiter said. "Vodka martini, straight up." He put down the drinks, and then hesitated. "Sir," he said, "I'm sorry about what happened."

"That's okay," I said.

"But I *do* have to check, sir, it's the law."

"Fine," I said.

"And the lady *did* look to be underage."

"Uh-huh, fine," I said.

"I hope you understand, sir."

"I do, yes."

"Is there anything else you'd like, sir, before I see to my other tables?"

"Yes, bring us another round when you get a chance, will you?"

"I'll take care of that right away, sir, before I see to my other tables."

"Fine, thank you."

"And I'm sorry about the misunderstanding, sir."

"That's okay."

"And sorry to have caused *you* any embarrassment, Miss."

"I'm not embarrassed," Jennifer said.

"Okay then," the waiter said, and grinned in relief. "Everything's okay then, good," he said, and went off to get the other drinks.

Jennifer lifted her glass. Without a word, she clicked it against mine and then sipped at the scotch. "Mmm, delicious," she said. She smiled suddenly. "I'm glad we ran into each other, you know, Mr. Eisler? We have a lot of talking to do."

"Oh? What about?"

"The abortion."

I lifted my glass again and took a deep swallow. "Jennifer," I said, "I really don't think we need to talk about your abortion."

"It was *your* abortion, too."

"No, it was my son's abortion. Yours and Adam's. Not mine."

"*You* paid for it," Jennifer said.

"I know I did. But that was three years ago, Jennifer. And it all worked out fine for everyone concerned. So, if it's okay with you, I'd really rather not . . ."

"Oh, sure," she said, and smiled. "What *would* you like to talk about, Mr. Eisler?"

"Anything," I said, "anything at all. How do you like Berkeley?"

"I like it a lot. I mean, I'm not into any of that protest stuff anymore, I'm a little too old for that . . ."

"Old?" I said, and laughed.

"Well, I mean, you can go around getting your face

74

smashed by The Establishment just so many times, you know what I mean? When you get to be my age, it's easier to go back to the apartment, kick off your shoes and bust a joint."

"Mmm-huh," I said.

"Marijuana," she said.

"Yes, I know."

"I thought maybe . . ."

"No, I understood you."

"But you disapprove, huh?"

"What gives you that idea?"

Jennifer shrugged and brushed hair out of her eyes. "I don't know. Your voice sounded kind of funny."

"I'm aware that all the kids today smoke marijuana."

"Can't bring yourself to call it pot, huh?"

"I'm afraid that wouldn't be very honest on my part."

"Oh, are you honest, Mr. Eisler?"

"I think I am."

"Was the abortion honest?" Jennifer asked, and the waiter came with our second round.

"Here we go, sir," he said. "Scotch on the rocks, vodka martini, straight up. I'm going to leave you now for just a few minutes to get some of those *hot hors d'oeuvres* from the serving tray. Would you like some hot *hors d'oeuvres*, Miss?"

"Yes, that would be very nice, thank you."

"I'll be back in just a little bit," the waiter said, and smiled, and hurried off.

I decided I had better lead the conversation where *I* wanted it to go, rather than entrusting it to Jennifer's direction. I was no more interested in discussing her abortion than I was in discussing my own appendectomy—less so, in fact. And yet, as I asked her about the courses she was taking and listened to the answers she gave, another conversation threaded itself through my mind and through the discussion we were presently engaged in, my son Adam coming to us in the living room just as John and Louis Garrod were saying goodnight, my son's blue eyes searching my face, scrub beard growing in patchily, long hair trailing like a Sienese page's— "Dad, I'd like to talk to you a minute, please."

And Abby jokingly saying to him, "Adam, if you're going to tell us that Jennifer's pregnant, please let it wait till morning, this has been a busy day," and John and Louise laughing.

And Adam smiling with his mouth but not his eyes and then asking me again, gently but insistently, if I would please come to his room because there was something important he wanted to discuss with me.

In his room (and all of this rushed through my mind as Jennifer opposite me now sipped at her scotch and started telling me about a *really* great professor at the school), Adam sat on the edge of his bed and said, flat out, "Dad, Jennifer's two weeks late, and we think she's pregnant." And I remember thinking how wonderful it was that my son could talk so honestly to his father, what was all this crap about a generation gap? And I remember telling him there was no need to worry yet, why when I was his age I had sweated out a dozen similar scares, and he told me, "Dad, Jennifer's *never* been late before." And I remember assuring him that perhaps her own anxiety was causing the delay, thinking all the while how proud I was of this marvelous open discussion I was having with my son, and convinced in my own mind of course that Jennifer was *not* pregnant, Jennifer could *not* be pregnant.

But Jennifer was.

". . . near the school," she said now. "Are you familiar with San Francisco?"

"Not really."

76

"Then the address wouldn't mean anything to you."

"No, it wouldn't. Do you live alone?"

"I've got two roommates."

"Berkeley girls?"

"Marcie's at Berkeley, yes. Paul's in the construction business."

"Oh," I said.

"Disapprove of *that*, too, huh?"

"Why should I?"

"You shouldn't, actually. Marcie and Paul have been making it together for almost a year and a half now. There's nothing wrong with them living together."

"I didn't say there was."

"I mean, I *do* have my own room and everything, you know. We're not like having a mass orgy up there, if that's what you're thinking."

"I'm not thinking anything of the sort," I said, and picked up my drink. Jennifer was studying me, and I was uncomfortably aware of her gaze.

"It's *just* what you're thinking," she said. "Well, you happen to be wrong. Paul's like a brother to me. I mean, we all walk around the apartment in our underwear, for God's sake. It's not what you think." She paused, searching for a clincher. "Paul even urinates with the bathroom door open," she said.

"I see," I said.

"It isn't what you think at all."

"Apparently not."

Jennifer suddenly began laughing.

"What?" I said.

"I just thought of something very funny."

"What is it?"

"Well, Marcie got a call from home just before the Spring

break, you know? From her mother, you know? Who wanted to know what her plans were, and all that. I took the call, you see, and I knew that Marcie and Paul were in the bedroom, you know, *doing* it, you know. So I carried the phone in—we've got this real long extension cord—and there's Paul on top of her, and I handed the phone to Marcie, and I said, 'It's for you, dear. It's your mother.' " Jennifer burst out laughing again. "What a great girl! Do you know what she did? She took the phone, Paul still on top of her and not missing a beat, and she went into this long conversation with her mother about plane connections and reservations and some new clothes she'd bought—oh God, it was *hilarious!*"

"Yes, it does sound very comical."

"You disapprove, right?"

"I'm not your father," I said. "I wish you'd stop asking me whether I approve or disapprove."

"I sometimes *used* to think of you as my father," Jennifer said. "When Adam and I were still in high school, and I used to come over all the time. My own father's a son of a bitch, you know. Getting him to say two straight words in a row is like expecting the Sphinx to do a eulogy on Moishe Dayan. Well, you remember how he was when we learned I was pregnant."

"I thought he handled it pretty well," I said, and then quickly changed the subject again. "You said Paul was in the construction business. What does he do?"

"He's an electrician. He's not a kid, you understand."

"No, I didn't understand that."

"Oh, God, he's almost as old as you are. How old are you?"

"Forty-one."

"Well, no, he's not quite *that* old."

"Nobody's quite that old," I said.

"Well, *you* are," Jennifer said, and drained her glass. "Do you think we can have another one of these? Paul's only thirty-nine, I guess. Or forty. I'm not sure. I'll have to ask him when I get home."

"Home?"

"San Francisco. The apartment."

"I see."

"That's home," Jennifer said simply, and I signaled for the waiter. He hurried over with the *hors d'oeuvres* he had promised, looking harried and apologetic.

"Sorry to have taken so long with these, sir," he said, "but I had some calls for drinks and I . . ."

"That's quite all right," I said. "We'd like another round, too, when you get a chance."

"Yes, sir," he said, "right away. In the meantime, we've got these nice little cocktail franks, and these little hot cheese patties, and some of these things wrapped in bacon here, I don't know what you call them. Enjoy yourselves, folks."

"Thank you," I said.

"I'll get those drinks for you," he said, and rushed off.

Jennifer picked up one of the tiny frankfurters and popped it into her mouth. "Mmmm," she said, "delicious. I'm starved to death, I may eat the whole damn platter."

"Maybe we ought to leave here and get some dinner," I said.

"What?"

"I said maybe we can have dinner together."

Jennifer nodded. She nodded and looked into her empty glass. Then she turned to me, and stared directly into my eyes, and said, "What you *really* mean, Mr. Eisler, is maybe we can go to bed together. Isn't that what you *really* mean?"

I stared back at her. She was a beautiful young girl in a strange town, and my wife was seven hundred air miles away

on a fire escape with the head of creation. Moreover, my own
son had been making love to her regularly when they were
both still in high school, she'd been pregnant at least once to
my knowledge, she had undergone an abortion for which I
had paid a thousand dollars, and she was now running
around in her bra and panties in an apartment with a forty-
year-old man who urinated with the door open. I did not honestly know whether I wanted to take her to dinner or take her
to bed.

"*Isn't* that what you'd really like to do, Mr. Eisler?"

"Maybe," I said, and smiled.

"Be honest. I'm twenty-one years old, well beyond the age
of consent."

"Are you consenting?"

"Are you asking?"

I didn't answer. I picked up my drink. The glass was
empty. I looked toward the bar for the waiter.

"Go ahead, Mr. Eisler. Ask me."

"I don't think I will," I said.

"Why not?"

"Maybe because you still call me Mr. Eisler."

Jennifer laughed and said, "What *shall* I call you? Sam?
That's your name, isn't it?"

"Yes, my name is Sam."

"I prefer Mr. Eisler. Come on, Mr. Eisler. Ask me."

The waiter brought our third round and put the drinks on
the table. He seemed about to leave us. Then he hesitated,
turned back, and said, "I'm certainly glad we cleared up our
misunderstanding, sir."

"Yes, I am, too."

"One thing I hate to do is irritate a customer. You realize,
though, that I *have* to ask for identification if somebody looks
underage. Otherwise . . ."

"Yes, I understand your position," I said.

"Otherwise, like suppose I serve some kid and we happen to have the law in here, why we could lose our liquor license just like that."

"Yes, of course you could."

"Listen," Jennifer said suddenly and sharply; "why don't you leave us alone? We're trying to talk here."

"What?" the waiter said.

"What?" Jennifer mimicked.

"I'm sorry, I just . . ."

"Don't be so sorry, just leave."

The waiter's jaw was hanging open. He looked at Jennifer in hurt surprise, and then turned to me for support. I busied myself with the hot cheese patties. The waiter shrugged, picked up his tray, and started walking back toward the bar, slowly, his shoulders slumped.

"You didn't have to do that," I said. "He was only . . ."

"He was a pain in the ass," Jennifer said. She picked up her fresh drink, drained half of it in a single swallow, and then said, "I never *did* thank you for the abortion, did I?"

"There was no need . . ."

"Oh, I'd *like* to thank you, Mr. Eisler."

"All right, so thank me."

"Thank you."

"You're welcome. Now let's . . ."

"And I think *you* ought to thank *me*," Jennifer said.

"I thank you," I said, and gave her a small nod.

"No, Mr. Eisler, you can *really* thank me."

There was something suddenly hard and cold and dangerous in her voice. I turned toward her on the leatherette seat, our knees touched, she moved hers away instantly. I searched her face and found her eyes.

"Thank you for what?" I asked.

81

"For going through with it. For not causing any trouble."

"Jennifer," I said, "there was never any question of you and Adam getting married. *You* didn't want it, *he* didn't want it, your *parents* didn't want it . . ."

"I don't recall anybody ever asking us."

"It was our understanding . . ."

"I loved your son," Jennifer said.

"It was our understanding . . ."

"Oh, the hell with you and your understanding," she said. "Nobody asked us what *we* wanted. Everybody just assumed we were too young, and too stupid, and too uncommitted . . ."

"Nobody forced you into anything."

"Everybody forced us into *everything!*" Jennifer said flatly.

"Look," I said, "we discussed this completely at the time. It was our understanding that you and Adam *wanted* the abortion."

"I loved that goddamn son of yours," she said, and suddenly she was crying.

My first reaction was to look quickly around the bar. The only person watching us was the waiter. I turned to Jennifer, covered her hand with my own, and said, "Don't, Jennifer. Please."

"I can cry if I want to," she said.

"All right, cry. But here, take this, dry your eyes . . ."

"We shouldn't have told you," she said. "*Keep* your damn handkerchief!"

"Jennifer, please!"

"We should have gone off and got married and never told any of you about it."

"Okay, but that's not what . . ."

"We should have known better. You're all full of crap, each and every one of you. Honest Sam Eisler. Sends an eighteen-year-old kid to Puerto Rico for an abortion! I was only *eighteen!* Damn it, I don't *want* your fucking handkerchief!" she said, and shoved my hand aside.

The waiter materialized again. He was wearing a stern and ominous look. He studied me solemnly for a moment and then said, "This person bothering you, Miss?"

Without looking up at him, Jennifer said, "No, *you're* bothering me! Would you please go away and leave us alone?"

"Because if he is, Miss . . ."

"Oh, my *God!*" Jennifer said.

"If he is . . ."

Jennifer suddenly seized my hand fiercely and looked up at the waiter, her eyes glistening, her face streaming tears. "This man is my lover," she said. "We meet . . ."

"Him?" the waiter said.

"*Him,* yes! We meet here secretly at the Chicago airport, and now you're ruining everything for us." She rose suddenly. "Come on, Sam," she said, "let's get out of here," and walked swiftly away from the table. I paid the check while the waiter apologized yet another time, and then I collected the luggage, and carried it in two trips to where Jennifer was waiting outside the bar. Her face was dry. Her eyes still glistened.

"Well," she said, "thank you for the drinks, Mr. Eisler."

"I think I prefer Sam," I said.

"Sure," she said. "Sam." She nodded, and then said, "Played your cards right, Sam, you could have had yourself a gay old time here in Chicago."

"Never was a good card player," I said.

"Not even in the old days, Mr. Eisler. Not even when two scared kids came to you and asked for advice. It's a shame you didn't understand what they needed from you."

"What did they need, Jennifer?"

"They *didn't* need an abortion, Mr. Eisler."

"Maybe they should have *asked* for what they needed."

"Maybe you should have *known* what they needed."

"I'm sorry I didn't," I said. "I mean that, Jennifer."

"No sorrier than I, Mr. Eisler," she said, and her voice caught, and I was sure she would begin crying again. But instead she picked up first one suitcase, and then the other, and then the wig box, and tossed her bag back over her shoulder, and brushed her hair away from her face, and walked off to try to catch a flight back to San Francisco, which was home.

The Sharers

I'm colored.

My wife Adele says that if I had ever really made peace with myself, as I keep telling her I have, I would not refer to myself as "colored." Instead, I would say, "I'm black" or "I'm a Negro," but never "I'm colored." This reasoning stems from the fact that her father was a very light Jamaican who, when he came to this country referred to himself constantly as "a person of color." Adele is very conscious of any such attempt at masquerade, though I have never heard her refer to herself as a "Negress," which term she finds derogatory. She also goes to the beauty parlor once a week to have her hair straightened, but she says this is only to make it more manageable, and disavows any suggestion that she does it to look more like a white woman. She, like her father, is very light.

For Adele's benefit, and to correct any possible misunderstanding, I hereby state that I am a colored black Negro. I was born and raised in a little town near St. Petersburg, Florida, and the only racial discomfort I ever experienced was when I was still coming along and was walking with my sister over a little wooden bridge leading somewhere, I didn't know where, and a gang of white kids attacked me. They did not touch my sister. They beat me up and sent me home crying. When my grandmother asked me why I had been so foolish as to attempt walking over that particular bridge, I said, "I wanted to see what was on the other side."

I left home in 1946 to attend Fordham University in New York, where I majored in accounting. I got my degree in June of 1950, and was immediately shipped to Korea. I met a lot of different people there, black and white, Northerner and Southerner, and the only problems I had were trying to stay warm, and fed, and alive. I will tell you more about that later. I met Adele in 1953, when I was discharged, and shortly after that I got the job with Goldman, Fish and Rutherford. I still work there. Adele and I were married in October of 1954, and we now have one child, a daughter named Marcia who is eleven years old and is having orthodontic work done. I tell you all this merely to provide some sort of background for what happened with Harry Pryor.

I had always thought of myself as a reasonable man, you see. I am thirty-eight years old and whereas it infuriates me whenever I hear a racial slur, I still don't think I would go to the South to do civil rights work. I'm very content with what I have. A good marriage, a good job, a daughter who is going to be a beauty once she gets rid of her braces, a house in North Stamford, and many many friends, some of whom are white.

In fact, everyone in my train group is white. I usually catch the 8:01 express from Stamford, which arrives at 125th Street in New York at 8:38. That's where I get off. The train continues on down to Grand Central, but I get off at 125th Street because Goldman, Fish and Rutherford has its offices on 86th and Madison, and it would be silly for me to go all the way downtown only to head back in the other direction again. There are generally six or seven fellows in the train group, depending on who has missed the train on any given morning. We always meet on the platform. I don't know where the 8:01 makes up, but when it reaches Stamford there are still seats, and we generally grab the first eight on either side of the aisle coming into the last car. We carry containers

86

of coffee with us, and donuts or coffee cake, and we have a grand time eating our breakfast and chatting and joking all the way to New York.

The morning I met Harry Pryor, I spilled coffee on his leg.

He is white, a tall person with very long legs. He has a mustache, and he wears thick-lensed glasses that magnify his pale blue eyes. He is about my age, I would guess, thirty-eight or nine, something like that. What happened was that I tripped over his foot as I was taking my seat, and spilled half a container of coffee on him, which is not exactly a good way to begin a relationship. I apologized profusely, of course, and offered him my clean handkerchief, which he refused, and then I sat down with the fellows. None of them seemed to mind Harry being there among us. I myself figured he was a friend of one of the other fellows. He didn't say anything that first morning, just listened and smiled every now and then when somebody told a joke. I got off at 125th Street, as usual, and took a taxi down to 86th Street.

You may think it strange that a fellow who earns only two hundred dollars a week, and who has a twenty-thousand-dollar mortgage on his house, and a daughter who is costing a fortune to have her teeth straightened, would be so foolish as to squander hard-earned money on a taxicab to and from the New York Central tracks, and only a single express stop from 86th Street. Why, you ask, would a working man allow himself the luxury of a taxi ride every morning and every night, which ride costs a dollar plus a twenty-five cents tip each way, when the subway costs considerably less? I'll tell you why.

When I was a soldier in Korea, I was very hungry and very cold most of the time. Also, I almost got shot. So I decided if ever I was lucky enough to become a civilian again, I would not deny myself any little luxuries that might make life more comfortable or more interesting or even just more bearable.

The first luxury I did not deny myself was buying Adele a two-carat engagement ring that cost me thirty-five hundred dollars, which was every penny I had managed to save during the war. Anyway, that's why I take a taxicab every morning. And every night, too. I like to pamper myself. When you've almost been shot once or twice, you begin to realize you'd better enjoy whatever time you have left on this good sweet earth of ours.

The next time I saw Harry, he was carrying a container of coffee, and he looked exactly like the rest of us. He took one of the seats we usually reserved for the group, and made a little joke about my not spilling coffee on him this morning, please. I laughed because I still thought he was somebody's friend. In fact, we all laughed. This encouraged him to tell a joke about two guys in the men's room, which was really a pretty good joke. I got off as usual at 125th, and Harry said goodbye to me when all the other fellows did. I took my taxicab downtown, smoked a cigar, and read my newspaper.

The next morning, Harry got off at 125th Street, too.

Now, I don't know whether or not you're familiar with this particular section of New York City. It is Harlem. On one corner, there's a big red brick building that must have been an armory at one time. There's a luncheonette on the opposite corner, and a newsstand and a Loft's on one side under the overhead tracks, and a hot dog stand on the other side. If you come straight out onto 125th Street and stand on Park Avenue waiting for a taxicab, you're out of luck. Every commuter who was on the train comes rushing down the steps to grab for cabs with both hands, it's a regular mob scene. So what I usually do is walk a block north, up to 126th Street, and I wait on the corner there, which is similar to shortstopping the chow line, an old trick I learned in Korea, where I was hungry all the time.

Harry and I came down the steps together that morning, but I immediately started for 126th Street, not asking him where he was going because I figured it was none of my business. He usually rode the train in to Grand Central, but here he was getting off at 125th, and I didn't know what to think. Maybe he had a girl up there in Harlem or something, I didn't know, and I wasn't asking. All I was interested in doing was getting a taxicab because it can get pretty chilly standing on 126th Street and Park Avenue in January. I got my taxi within five minutes, and I sat back and lit my cigar, but as I passed the next corner, I noticed that Harry was still standing there trying to get a cab for himself. I didn't ask the driver to stop for him, but I made a mental note of it, which I forgot soon enough because Harry didn't get off at 125th again until maybe two or three weeks later.

This was already the beginning of February, and Park Avenue up there in Harlem looked pretty bleak. It is not like Park Avenue down around 80th Street, if that's what you thought. Harlem is a ghetto, you see, with crumbling tenements and garbage-strewn backyards. I have even seen rats the size of alley cats leaping across the railroad tracks on 125th Street, bigger than the ones I saw in Korea. But in the winter, in addition to everything else, the place gets a bleak forbidding look. You just know, in the winter, that there are people shivering inside those crumbly buildings, afraid to come out because it's even colder in the streets. You can stand a ghetto in the spring, I guess, because you can walk outside and look up at the sky. In New York, there is a sky above the building tops, and it is often a beautiful blue sky, even in a ghetto. But in the winter, you are trapped. There is only you and the four walls and the extra heat you can maybe get from a kerosene burner. I never go through Harlem in the winter without thinking how lucky I am.

I was standing on the corner of 126th and Park, when Harry Pryor walked up to me and said, "Are you taking a cab downtown?"

"Yes," I said, "I take one every morning."

"To where?" he asked.

"To 86th and Madison."

"Well," he said, "I'm going down to 84th and Park. Shall we share a cab?"

"Why not?" I said, first big mistake.

We got into the taxi together, and I asked him if he minded if I smoked a cigar, explaining that it was my habit to have a cigar on the way down to work each morning. He said he didn't mind at all, in fact he liked the smell of a good cigar, so I offered him the cigar I would have smoked after lunch and, thank God, he refused it.

"What sort of work do you do, Howard?" he asked, and I told him I was an accountant, stop in some time and I'll figure out your income tax for you. He laughed, and then coughed politely when I lit my cigar. He opened the window a little, which I really didn't need as it was probably eighty degrees below zero outside, with Harlem looking gray and bleak and barren as the taxi sped past the market on Park Avenue, the push carts on our right, the sidewalk shopkeepers bundled in mufflers and heavy overcoats, salesgirls wearing galoshes, little school kids rushing across the avenue to disappear under the stone arches that held up the New York Central tracks.

"What sort of work do you do?" I asked, beginning to feel the breeze from the window, and wanting to ask him to close it, but also wondering whether he might not then choke on my cigar. As you can see, my troubles had already started.

"I'm in the travel business," he said. "I'm a partner in a travel agency." I didn't say anything. I had never met a travel agent before. The one time I took Adele to Bermuda, I had made all the reservations myself. Adele had said it was a luxury we could not afford. I told Adele there are certain luxuries you *have* to afford, or you wither away and die. This was before Marcia's monumental dental work had begun, of course. I sometimes think that child will have braces on her teeth the day she gets married.

"Yessir," Harry said, "we've got two offices, one on 45th and Lex, and the other up here on 84th. I spend my time shuttling between the two of them."

"Well, that must be very interesting work," I said, "being a travel agent."

"Oh yes, it's very stimulating," Harry said, "do you mind if I open this window?" The window, it seemed to me, was *already* open, but without waiting for my answer, Harry rolled it all the way down. I thought I would freeze to death. It was plain to see that he had never been to Korea.

"Listen," I said, "would you like me to put out this cigar?"

"Oh no," he said, "I enjoy the smell of a good cigar."

Then why are you freezing us out of this cab, I thought, with the window open, I thought, like an icebox in here, I thought, but did not say. I was very happy to see the New York Central tracks disappear underground because that meant we had already reached 98th Street, and I could get out of the cab very soon and run upstairs to the office, where I knew it was warm because Dave Goldman always kept the heat at eighty degrees, and wore a sweater under his jacket besides. The driver, whose head was hunched down into his shoulders now because he too was beginning to feel the wintry blast, made a right turn on 86th and pulled to a stop on the corner of Madison Avenue. I told him to hold his flag, and then I took out my wallet and handed Harry a dollar and a quarter, which is exactly what the ride cost me every morning, and which I was, of course, more than willing to pay for having had the pleasure of being frozen solid.

Harry said, "Please."

"No, take it," I said. "I ride a cab every morning, and this is what it costs me, so you might . . ."

"No, no," Harry said.

"Look, we agreed to share a taxi. I can't let you pay . . ."

"Traveling is my business," Harry said. "I'll charge it to the agency." He smiled under his black mustache. His pale blue eyes crinkled behind his glasses. "It's deductible, you should know that."

"Well, I feel kind of funny," I said, and thrust the money at him again. But he held out his hand, palm downward, and then gently nudged the offer away, as though the money had germs.

"I insist," he said.

"Well, okay," I said, and shrugged, and said, "Thank you, have a nice day," and got out of the cab and ran for the office. It took me a half-hour to get my circulation back.

The next morning, Harry got off at 125th Street again, and again he said, "Care to share a taxi?" so what could I say? Could I say, Listen, my friend, I like to ride alone in the morning, I like to smoke my cigar with the windows closed, you understand, closed very *tight* against the cold outside, not even open a crack, with cigar smoke floating all around me, reading my newspaper, nothing personal, you understand, no hard feelings, but that's one of my little luxuries, that's what I promised myself in Korea many many years ago, could I tell that to the man?

I suppose I could have, but I didn't.

Instead, I got into the taxi with him, and I lit a cigar for myself; and he immediately opened the window. So I immediately snuffed out the cigar and asked him if he would please close the window.

"How's the travel business these days?" I asked. I had folded my arms across my chest, because I was in a pretty surly mood. What I usually do, you see, is ration out my cigars, one in the morning in the taxi on the way to work, another one after lunch, another one in the taxi on the way back from work, and the last one after dinner. Four cigars a day, that's enough. I do twenty pushups each morning, and twenty before I go to bed, to keep the old "bod" in shape, as my daughter calls it. She kills me, that girl. So I was thinking I really didn't *need* this guy to ride down with me and deprive me of my cigar, who needed him? But there he was, telling me all about the travel business and about a charter flight they were getting up to Aspen, Colorado (just the *thought* of Aspen, Colorado, gave me the chills) and had I ever tried skiing?

"No," I said, "I have never tried skiing. I don't even like ice skating."

"That's too bad, Howard," he said, "I think you would find skiing a most agreeable sport."

"Well," I said, "I'm too old to go out and break a leg. When a man gets set in his ways, he develops certain habits, you know, that he doesn't like to change," hoping he would realize I was talking about my morning cigar, which he didn't.

"That's true," he said, "but you seem to be in pretty good shape, and I doubt if you would break a leg."

"My cousin broke a leg in his own bathtub," I said.

"I'm sorry to hear that," Harry said. "Did you know they shot *The Pawnbroker* on this corner?"

"Which pawnbroker?" I asked, not having heard about any shooting on that corner, which was the comer of 116th Street and Park Avenue.

"The movie," Harry said.

"Oh, the movie. I didn't see that movie."

"It was a very good movie," Harry said. "They shot it right on this corner."

I was really wanting a cigar very badly by that time. I looked out at the El Radiante bar and visualized *Harry* being shot on the corner.

"There were a lot of your people in that picture," Harry said.

"My people?" I said.

"Negroes," he said.

"Oh," I said.

"It was a very good picture."

The cab sped downtown. The overhead tracks came level with the ground, then sank below the pavement and disappeared. When we reached 86th Street, I took out a dollar and a quarter again and thrust it into Harry's hand, but he turned his hand over quickly and let the money fall onto the seat.

"Nossir," he said, "not on your life. I have to go down this way, anyway."

"But I have to go down this way, too," I complained.

"Can *you* charge it to the business?"

"No, but . . ."

"Then don't be silly." He picked up the money and stuffed it into my coat pocket. "Now go ahead, don't be silly, Howard."

"Well, thank you," I said, "I appreciate it," and then realized I didn't even know his name, I had never heard anyone calling him by name on the train. "Thank you," I said again, and got out of the cab.

We have a small office, and Concetta, our secretary, has asthma, which means that smoking a cigar and filling the air with deadly fumes would give her coughing fits all day long. So I stood in the corridor outside the men's room and smoked my morning cigar there. Rafe Goldman came in at nine-thirty. I was still standing there smoking. He fanned the air with both huge hands and said, "Whooosh, you trying to fumigate the place?"

"Well, I know Concetta doesn't like cigar smoke," I said.

"You can smell that the minute you get off the elevator," Rafe said. "What is that, an El Ropo?" he said, and nudged me, and laughed.

"It's a good cigar," I said. "Cost me twenty-five cents."

"We're going to have complaints from the Fire Department," Rafe said, and laughed again. "They'll probably send the commissioner around."

"Look," I said, a bit heatedly, "if I can't smoke it in the office, and if I can't smoke it here in the corridor outside the men's room where it isn't bothering anybody, where the hell *can* I smoke it?"

"Don't get excited," Rafe said, and patted my arm. "Why don't you go smoke it downstairs?"

Downstairs was a hundred below zero, downstairs was troikas followed by packs of starving gray wolves.

Rafe went into the men's room. I put out the cigar and went inside to my desk. All that morning, I thought about Harry. You have to understand that whereas I appreciated his having paid my cab fare on two separate occasions, I would have preferred paying my *own* damn fare so that I could have smoked my cigar in peace without a fresh air fiend in attendance. I stress this point only because Adele later said perhaps I was really a Cheap Charlie who *enjoyed* having my cab fare paid each morning. This simply was not true, and I told Adele so in very positive terms. For whereas things are sometimes a bit tight in North Stamford, what with Marcia's tooth alignment and all, I can certainly afford to pay my own cab fare. In fact, as I pointed out, and as Adele well knew, the taxi rides to and from work were luxuries I felt I *owed* myself, essential elements of the private little party I had been throwing to celebrate the fact that I had not got killed in Korea.

So it seemed to me that Harry Pryor was sharing something more than just a taxi with me, and I decided to tell him flat out come Monday morning that whereas I enjoyed his company immensely, I really preferred riding down to work alone as it gave me a chance for contemplation, an opportunity to ease into the long hard day ahead, which was not exactly true, but which I rehearsed nonetheless all through the weekend. Then I remembered that I didn't even know his name, so I called Frank Cooperman on Sunday night to ask about it.

"Who do you mean?" he said.

"The fellow who rides in with us each morning."

"Which fellow?"

"The one with the black mustache and the blue eyes and the glasses. Who tells all the jokes in the morning."

"I think his name is Harry," Frank said.

"Don't you *know?*"

"Well, I'm not sure."

"He's your *friend,* isn't he?"

"No, no," Frank said. "*My* friend? What gave you that idea?"

"I just thought he was your friend," I said.

"I thought he was *your* friend," Frank said.

"Well, whose friend is he?" I asked.

"Search me," Frank said.

"Well, what's his last name?" I said.

"Pryor, I think."

"Thank you," I said, and hung up, a little annoyed with Frank, I'm not sure why. I debated whether I should call my taxi-mate "Mr. Pryor" (since he didn't seem to be anyone's friend) or just plain "Harry" when I broke the news to him, and then I rehearsed it both ways, figuring I'd play it by ear when the time came. I could barely sleep that night. Adele finally poked me in the ribs and said, "Howard, if you don't stop tossing, I'm going to go sleep in Marcia's room." I didn't answer her as she very often makes dire threats in her sleep. On Monday morning, I drove to the station, and there was Mr. Harry Pryor waiting on the platform with the other fellows, coffee container in one hand, wrapped cheese Danish in the other.

"Morning, Howard," he said.

"Morning, Harry," I said.

"Getting off at 125th as usual?" he asked.

"As usual," I said.

"Would you care to share a taxi with me?" he asked.

That was my opportunity, and I should have given him my rehearsed speech right then and there, but I didn't want to embarrass him in front of the other fellows. So I said, "Yes, Harry," and figured this would be our last shared ride together, I'd tell him how I felt on the way down to 86th.

It was a bitterly cold day.

Men were hunched over small coal fires in empty gasoline drums, girls clutched coat collars to their throats, icicles hung from awnings, broken orange crate slats jutted crookedly from frozen curbside puddles.

"I can't tell you how much I enjoy this morning ride with you, Howard," Harry said for openers.

I grunted.

"I don't know many Negroes," he said.

I didn't know what to say to that one, so I coughed.

"That's a bad cold you have there," Harry said.

I grunted again.

97

"You ought to quit smoking," he said.

"I have," I said. "Temporarily," and I thought now is the time to tell him. Right this minute. I turned toward him on the seat.

"How else can we get to know each other?" Harry said.

"I beg your pardon," I said.

"Negroes and whites," he said. "How else can we possibly breach the barricade?"

"Well," I said, thinking I didn't have any particular barricade to breach, and if Harry had one, he shouldn't attempt to breach it in a taxicab. "Actually . . ."

"Can I walk up to a Negro on the street and say, 'Listen, fellow, let's have a drink together, I'd like to know you people better.' Can I say that?"

I thought No, you had better not say *that*, Mr. Pryor, especially not up here in Harlem. I glanced through the window on my right where the city had put up a housing development. On one of the walls, a teenage letterer had painted the name of his club. He had spelled it wrong. For posterity, the words "The Redemers" boldly asserted themselves in white letters on the brick wall.

"So just having the opportunity to talk to you this way, to get to *know* you this way, is very important to me, Howard. I want to thank you for it. I want to tell you how much I appreciate your generosity."

"Yes, well," I said, "don't mention it, really."

I felt trapped, and frustrated, and suddenly in danger. Once, in Korea, when we were trying to take this hill, we had two of our guys with a mortar about a hundred yards on the left, and the sergeant and another guy and me with the mortar rounds over on the right. But we couldn't get to each other because the Chinese had set up a machine gun on top of the hill, and they kept raking the ground between us. It was very frustrating. Finally, somebody called for artillery to knock out the emplacement. But that was after the sergeant had already sent my buddy to get killed trying to lug the ammo across that hundred yards of bullet-sprayed ravine to where the mortar was waiting. The sergeant tapped me on the shoulder. I was next. Just then, the artillery barrage started. I don't know who called for the support, probably the captain of Baker company which was on a little knoll looking down into this depression where we were trapped and frustrated. I never found out. That was one of the times I almost got killed.

I felt the same frustration now as we rode down to 86th Street, and I also felt the same danger. That's ridiculous, I know. Harry was only sharing a taxicab with me. But I had the feeling he was also trying to move in on me, he had put all his furniture into a Santini Brothers van and now they were moving into my head and my heart and even my soul, and were beginning to unpack their barrels.

The cab pulled to the curb at Madison Avenue. I silently took out a dollar and a quarter and handed it to Harry.

"Please," he said.

"Are you sure this is on the business?" I asked.

"Absolutely," he said.

"Okay," I said, and shrugged, and put my money away, and got out of the cab. I didn't tell him to have a nice day. I just closed the taxi door, slammed it actually (the Negro cabbie turned to give me a dirty look), and then stopped for a cup of coffee before going up to the office.

That night, I had my talk with Adele, the one in which she insisted I was a Cheap Charlie. When I finally shouted that the cab fare had nothing to do with the damn situation, she very quietly said, "You're allowing a white man to buy your freedom and your privacy."

"That's not true."

"It *is* true, Howard."

"You're a racist, is what you are," I said. "You're as bad as the segregationists down south."

"He's going to ask you to have lunch with him one day, you wait and see."

"I don't *want* to have lunch with him."

"Do you want to share a taxi with him?"

"No!"

"But you *do* share one," Adele said. She nodded sagely. "And you'll have lunch with him, too, wait and see."

"I will *not* have lunch with him," I said.

"You're allowing him to enslave you," Adele said. "Howard, you are letting him snatch you out of the African jungle and throw you into the hold of a ship in chains."

"He wants to be my *friend!*"

"Do you want to be *his* friend?"

"No, but . . ."

"Are you afraid of him, Howard?"

"'No, but . . ."

"Then why can't you tell him you don't want to ride with him? I'll tell you why, Howard. You can't because he's white. And it's the white man's privilege to decide whether or not he'll ride with a nigger."

"Don't use that word in this house," I said.

"Howard," she said, "if you let Harry Pryor do this to you, you are nothing but a nigger," and she went up to bed.

I sat alone in the living room for a long time. Then I went upstairs and made sure Marcia hadn't kicked the blanket off the way she usually did. She was sleeping with a wide grin on her face. Her braces gleamed in the dim light from the hallway. I touched her face gently, tucked the blanket in around her feet, and then went into my own bedroom. Adele was asleep. A frilly cap covered her set hair. My grandmother had worn an old silk stocking on her head the day I came home from trying to walk over the bridge. The toe of the stocking, knotted, had flapped around her ears as she shook her head and washed my cuts.

My grandmother's father had been a slave.

I decided to tell Harry in the morning that I no longer cared to share a taxi with him.

I kept putting it off.

He got into the taxi with me every morning, and every morning I would turn toward him and start to tell him, and I would see those pale blue eyes behind the thick glasses, and I would remember how he had eased his way into our group on the train. And it would occur to me that perhaps Harry Pryor needed my companionship more than I needed my own privacy, which was crazy.

He kept asking me questions about Negroes.

He wanted to know how it felt to walk into a good restaurant, did I always fear I would be turned away, or not served, or otherwise treated badly? He wanted to know how I handled hotel reservations; did I explain on the phone that I was a Negro, or did I simply arrive with my luggage and surprise them? He asked me if I had ever gone out with white girls, so I told him about Susan who had been in the School of Journalism at Columbia and whom I had dated for six months when I was going to Fordham. We were quite open about being seen in public together, I told Harry, even though Susan never mentioned me to her parents, and even though I never wrote about her in my letters home. We had quite a thing going for six months, but then it all ended pretty routinely when I went off to fight in Korea. I wrote to her once or twice, and once or twice she answered, and then it simply ended, almost as if it had never happened at all.

I also told him about my sister who was in the English department at U.C.L.A., and how she had gone through a severe Muslim phase, only to swing over to dating white men exclusively. She was now involved in all that crazy California scene of surfing and psychedelics and Oriental religion. I told him she still called me "Hub," which had been my nickname as a boy. I told him Adele's brother favored a separate Negro nation, that he had been jailed six times in Georgia and Alabama, and that he had fled north this past summer after striking back at a deputy with a piece of lead pipe. His eyes burn in his head, I said, I think he's a fanatic. I told him that I myself had respected only Martin Luther King as leader of the civil rights movement, but that I would never ride a freedom bus or join in a march because, quite frankly, I was afraid I would be hurt or possibly killed. I told him I had an aunt named Florina who hired out as a cleaning woman, and whom I had not seen since I was coming along in the South, though every Christmas she sent a plum cake to the house in North Stamford. I told him that James Baldwin gave me a pain in the ass. And at last, I told him about what had happened the day I tried to walk across that little wooden bridge a mile from where my sister and I lived with my grandmother.

"Why didn't you fight back?" Harry asked.

"I was just a little kid," I said.

"How old?"

"Six. And my sister was only four."

"Did they hurt you?"

"Yes."

"What did you think?"

"I thought I was a fool to get into a fight with bigger kids."

"Bigger *white* kids?"

"No."

"But you *must* have thought that, Howard."

"No, I didn't," I said. "Just *bigger* kids, that's all. White had nothing to do with it."

These conversations all took place in various taxicabs in the space of, oh, two or three weeks, I would guess. All the time, I had the oddest feeling that Harry was waiting for me to say something I had not yet said, reveal something I had kept hidden until then, *do* something—it was the oddest feeling. It brought to mind again the Chinese machine gunners waiting for us to try a run through that treacherous ravine.

One morning, as I got out of the cab, I realized I had forgotten to offer Harry my customary dollar and a quarter. I reached for my wallet.

"Forget it," he said.

"Harry," I said, "we've been riding together for a long time now. I wish you'd let me pay my share."

"It's deductible," he said, and shrugged.

"Are you sure?"

"I am absolutely positive," he said.

"Okay," I said, and got out of the cab. "So long," I said, "have a good day."

"The same to you, Howard," he answered. "The same to you."

All through the next week, I rode down to 86th Street in a cab with Harry, telling him what it was like to be a Negro in America. I no longer offered to pay for the ride because it seemed to me the point had been settled. If he really was deducting it, then why go through the same pointless routine each morning, taking out my wallet and extending the cash only to have it turned away?

"Goodbye, Harry," I would say. "Thanks for the ride."

"My pleasure, Howard," he would answer, "my distinct

pleasure," and the taxi would gun away from the curb.

On the following Monday, I arrived at the Stamford station late, approaching the train from the front end, which was closest to where I always parked my car. The train was about to pull out, so I hopped aboard and began walking back toward the last car when suddenly something powerful rooted me to the spot. I will not have to sit with the group, I thought, I will not have to ride in a taxi with Harry Pryor and tell him what it is like to be a Negro in America, I will not have to do either of those things if I stay up here in the first car. If I stay up here, I thought, if I take a seat up here, then I may be able to ride a taxicab down to 86th all by myself, light a cigar and inhale some good luxurious smoke, read my newspaper in peace and quiet, ruminate upon the state of world affairs if I want to, or dream of belly dancers in Cairo if I want to, or pray for peace, or wonder about my daughter's teeth, or think about my wife's car, or sketch out some plans for a boat I'd like to build one day, what with the Sound being so close and all. In short, if I take a seat in this first car of the train, I can perhaps avoid Harry at 125th Street and therefore *be* a Negro in America.

I took a seat next to a fat woman wearing a horrible perfume. I felt like a defector. I was certain they would come looking for me before the train reached 125th Street, certain Harry would burst into the car and shout, "Ah-ha, *there* you are!" exposing me for the runaway slave I most certainly was. The train rumbled across the Harlem River Bridge, the bleak gray tenements appeared suddenly on the horizon. I pulled my collar up high, and leaped onto the platform. I saw Harry as he got off the train at the other end, but I pretended not to. Instead, I walked very quickly to the closest staircase, raced down it, and, rather than walking up to 126th Street, cut across Park Avenue and headed crosstown.

I had just reached Lexington Avenue when two things happened at once.

A pair of taxis came rolling toward the corner, and I saw Harry Pryor standing there with his arm raised, hailing one of them. He saw me in that same instant.

"Good morning, Howard," he said quickly, and pulled open the door of the nearest taxi. "I'll grab this one," he said, and got into the cab hastily and slammed the door. The second taxi had just pulled to the curb. I opened the door and got in. "86th and Madison," I said, and watched as the taxi ahead, the one carrying Harry, gunned away from the curb and headed downtown.

I did not know what to think at first.

Had he realized I'd been trying to duck him, had he walked over to Lexington Avenue only to make it easier for me, figuring I'd head for my usual post at 126th and Park? Or had I offended him in some manner, had I said something the week before that had caused him to make a simultaneous and identical decision: we would no longer ride with each other, we would no longer share.

And then I realized what it was.

I had at last done the thing Harry had been waiting for me to do all along. After all that talk, after all those explanations and revelations and confidences freely offered, I had at last managed to convey to Harry the certain knowledge that I was only, at best, a Negro. I had finally and unprotestingly accepted his generosity, only to become in that instant the white man's burden. I had made the terrible mistake, again, of thinking I could walk across that bridge with immunity, allow Harry to pay my fare at last because, you see, I was an equal who understood all about tax deductions, an accountant, you see, an educated man—even perhaps, a friend.

It was not a cold day, it was the middle of March, and

spring was on the way, but I felt a sudden chill and longed to join the old men still huddling over coal fires in the side streets of Harlem. At 86th Street, I gave the driver a dollar and a quarter and got out of the cab.

I had forgotten to light my cigar.

Since that day, I have avoided Harry by taking an earlier train, the 7:30 out of Stamford, which arrives at 125th Street at 8:20. This gives me a little extra time, so I no longer have to ride a taxi to work in the morning. Instead, I walk over to Lexington Avenue, and I board the downtown express there on a platform that is thronged with Negroes like myself.

I do not mind it except when it's raining.

When it's raining, I think of Harry riding a cab downtown, alone, and I wonder if he has the window open a crack, and I wonder if anything will ever convince him that I was able to pay my own way, and that I would have happily done so if he'd only given me the chance.

The Couple Next Door

The closet was a big walk-in, far more storage space than we needed on such a short Caribbean vacation. After we'd folded our beachwear into three dresser drawers, there was little else to hang—Kara's two cocktail dresses, my own light-weight Navy blue blazer and gray slacks. We would be here for only five days, a brief respite from New York's brutal February.

"Honey?" the voice in the closet said. "Come take a look at *this!*"

Kara and I had come up from the beach at a quarter past four, and were napping before dinner time. The voice sounded so immediate I thought it was actually in the room with us. It was a male voice, young and obviously impressed by whatever it was he was asking "Honey" to come see. Startled out of a light sleep, it took me a moment to realize that the voice was coming from our closet, and another moment to comprehend that it was coming from beyond the closet wall.

"Someone's at the door," Kara mumbled.

"No, he's in the closet," I said.

"Mm, funny," she said.

We were both awakened an hour later by the sound of female moans, male groans, genderless gutter talk and heavy breathing. Kara sat up in a flash, directing a green-eyed laser beam at the closet, from beyond which the sounds of sexual engagement were emanating. Only once before in our twelve

107

years of married life had we overheard a man and a woman making love in another room. That was in the Connaught Hotel in London, at two A.M. on a moonlit night in May, the windows wide open, the tumultuous tossings and passionate cries of pleasure rising from across the courtyard. Oddly, when it was all over and the night was once again still, the woman kept repeating over and over again, like the heroine in a Victorian novel, "You, sir, are a blackguard," an epithet that reduced us both to helpless muffled laughter.

Here in the tropics, there was the sound of the ocean rushing the beach beyond our shuttered windows, and the whisper of palm fronds on the moonlit balmy night, and once again the same cries of passion spilling from the closet and across the room to where we lay listening, captive in our own bed.

We learned the next day that the object of attraction in the closet next door was an enormous tropical spider. From what we could overhear, and we overheard all, this was a truly extraordinary bug.

"God, he's gigantic, sweetie!"

"Just don't get too close, honey."

"Look at all those *colors!*"

"Is that green or blue?"

"Green *and* blue."

"Some red, too."

"Do you think he's poisonous?"

"I don't think so, honey."

"What shall we do with him?"

"What do you mean?"

"Well . . . should we spray him or something?"

"I don't think he'll hurt us."

"But let's hang our things away from that corner, okay?"

At which point, I swear to God, they both began clapping

their hands and singing "Eansie-Beansie Spider."

It wasn't as if either of us had secret lovers. There was no one else. Neither had we "outgrown" each other, as the cliché would have it. I'm an oboe player. I do sit-in work with whichever symphony orchestra has a musician out sick or otherwise unable to meet a performance date. That winter, I was playing on and off with the Philharmonic, but such work is rare, believe me. I usually play with far less distinguished orchestras here and there around the city. If you have occasion to look me up in a program sometime, I'm Richard Haig. I sit there in the woodwinds section, a pleasant-looking man in a black suit, in no way outstanding. I once played a Galway concert. That was truly exciting.

I don't know if you're familiar with very many children's book illustrators. I happen to know quite a few of them because that's what Kara does for a living. They're a particularly gentle breed, most of them with children of their own, though Kara and I haven't been blessed in that respect. She's thirty-seven years old, my wife, to my forty-two, a quite beautiful, soft-spoken blonde with a keen sense of humor and a lovely smile, particularly radiant now that she'd begun to tan. Perhaps the most flamboyant thing about her is her name. Cara, of course, means "dear" in Italian, but Kara's mother tacked a Teutonic K onto it, giving it a post-modernist twist that singled her out from every other little girl growing up in the sixties.

What I'm trying to say is that neither of us had progressed very far beyond the other in our twelve years of marriage. I had not achieved anything more important than Kara had. She had no real reason to feel threatened by me. She was happy with what she did, and had won no recognition that might have caused me to feel envious or resentful. There was no competition between us. We were equal partners, perfectly content with the people we were.

That's not what was wrong with our marriage.

I don't know what was wrong with it.

While Kara took long, solitary walks on the beach, I tried to determine which of the hotel guests were the two in the room next door. They were young, yes, or at least their voices sounded youthful. They were energetic, too, undeniably so. In addition to their clockwork afternoon matinees, Kara and I were treated to audio performances at midnight, and highly vocal encores just before breakfast. I figured they had to be honeymooners. But then, something Sweetie said—he was the male—changed my mind about that.

They were talking about a sweater they were searching for in the closet; the nights here in the tropics tended to get a bit chilly. Sweetie was trying to remember where they'd purchased it. It was clear that they'd been together on vacation someplace. Had it been Bali? South America? My interest was piqued. Kara and I had been to these places as well. Then Sweetie said, "I remember."

"Where?" Honey asked.

"Our fifth anniversary," Sweetie said.

"No, you bought me a coral necklace."

"This wasn't a gift. We were just walking along . . ."

"Paris!"

"The little shop on the L'Ile de la Cité."

"I remember," she said.

"Do you remember the Christmas Eve mass at Saint Suplice?"

"Yes, sweetie, I remember."

Not honeymooners then. Nor as young as I'd first surmised. Married for at least five years, perhaps longer. World travelers; from the sound of them. No clue as to what either of them did for a living. No clue as to whether or not there were children in the marriage. The only intimation I had of Honey's physical appearance was supplied by Sweetie one evening. Again, their voices came from the other side of the thin closet wall, floating into my unintentionally receptive ears. Or perhaps, like an amateur detective on the track of something big, I had became a deliberate listener, fascinated now by this couple who seemed so very much in love.

"Wear the blue," he suggested. "It's better with your hair. Especially now." And a pause. "You look so beautiful in blue."

Blue was a blonde's color. I assumed Honey's hair had turned lighter in the sun, as had Kara's.

I started watching for blondes.

Years ago, I forget how many, Kara and I used to play a game where we tried to determine whether any given tourist was an American or a foreigner. There were only two rules: we had to guess before we heard a person speak, and dining habits didn't count; we knew that foreigners cut their meat and forked it into their mouths without changing hands. We learned to look for facial expressions and hand gestures, the manner in which a person walked, hair styles, tailoring, shoes. To our amazement and delight, we were soon able to guess correctly at least eighty percent of the time. We used to play lots of games like that.

Now, while Kara walked the beach searching for shells, I periodically looked up from the biography I was reading to scan the faces of couples strolling past. I looked first for a blonde woman, and next for two people obviously in love with each other. The tropics did things to vacationers. There were smiles on sun-tanned faces. Every couple walking by seemed to be holding hands. Behind my sunglasses, I watched. The sun was strong. The ocean charged the shore repeatedly, retreated, encroached again. The palms swayed easily on the far horizon, there was a boat with blue sails. I dozed.

Kara awakened me some fifteen minutes later to exhibit the shells she'd collected, reddish-brown and cream-colored and stark white.

The hotel band played tunes from the forties.

The crowd here was a bit young for such dated fare, but the dance floor was an outdoor oval fringed with red bougain-villea, yellow hibiscus and purple jacaranda, and it lured dancers as surely as might have the rock and roll we grew up with. Here under the stars, couples clung to each other and swayed to swingless renditions of Glenn Miller arrangements. There were four or five blondes on the dance floor. Each danced with her eyes closed, tight in the circle of her partner's arms. I wondered if one of them was Honey.

Once, on La Costa Brava, I forget when, it must have been five or six years ago, Kara and I returned to the hotel after a midnight Spanish dinner and swept onto the dance floor like professional flamenco dancers. Everyone applauded.

"Kara?" I said. "Would you care to dance?"

"Thanks, Richard, no," she said. "The sun really knocked me out today."

I watched the couples swirling by.

In a little while, we went up to our room.

At two in the morning, I was awakened again by Honey and Sweetie. I lay still and silent in the dark, listening to their whispered words of love and shouted cries of passion.

Our short vacation ended the next day.

We checked out without ever seeing the couple next door.

On the plane home, Kara made tentative sketches for the new book she'd accepted, and I finished reading the biography I'd started. I must have napped. The captain's voice woke me up. I elevated my seat and turned to where Kara was still asleep. I touched her shoulder.

"Kara?" I said. "We're approaching Kennedy."

Her eyes fluttered open. She looked at me blankly.

And suddenly I knew who they were.

The couple next door.

They were us.

Long ago.

The Victim

An afternoon in October, ten years ago.

She was nineteen years old, and a storm broke just as she was leaving the Columbia campus. She tried to cover her head with her notebook, but she was soaked to the marrow within minutes. Standing helplessly in the middle of the sidewalk, not knowing whether to run back for the shelter of one of the buildings or ahead to the subway kiosk, she noticed a red Volkswagen at the curb, its door open. A young man was leaning across the front seat.

"Hey!" he shouted. "Get in before you drown!" Then, seeing the look of hesitation on her face, he immediately added, "I'm not a weirdo, I promise."

She got into the car.

"My name's Bobby Hollis," he said.

"How do you do, Bobby?"

"What's *your* name?"

"Laura Pauling."

"Laura and Bobby."

"Yes. Laura and Bobby."

Wide grin, mischievous blue eyes, straight brown hair a bit too carelessly combed, falling onto his forehead, long and lanky Bobby—oh, how the girls on campus went for Bobby! Laura had hooked herself a big one out there in the rain. A young man who'd been on the dean's list for three successive semesters, wrote a column for the school newspaper, played the lead in the drama group's presentation of *Arsenic and Old*

114

Lace, and also played the clarinet. "Would you like to hear the glissando passage at the beginning of 'Rhapsody in Blue'?" A young man who, most important of all, was absolutely crazy about—

Her.

Wow.

Little Laura Pauling. Five foot four, mousy brown hair that sort of matched her brown eyes. Fairly decent figure but not anything anyone in his right mind would rave about. Except Bobby Hollis, who maybe *wasn't* in his right mind.

Wow.

Laura had hooked herself the seventh wonder of the *world* out there in the rain. When at last he asked her to marry him, she accepted at once. Of *course,* she accepted! And before she knew it, she had two children who were surely the eighth and *ninth* wonders, and eventually she forgot what she'd been doing up there on that uptown campus. Forgot she'd been studying to . . . well, become something. Well, that wasn't important. Well, yes, it was important, but the hell with it.

Laura had been willing to go along with changing dirty diapers and wiping runny noses so long as she believed Bobby loved her. After all, somebody had to do those things while Bobby was busy making a career for himself. Somebody had to keep those old home fires burning while Bobby was out chasing—

Out chasing.

Period.

She learned about it from a well-meaning associate of his who'd had too many martinis.

"Laura," he'd said, "forgive me if I'm brutally frank, okay?"

"What is it, Dave?"

"I know a man's supposed to look the other way and keep

his mouth shut when a friend of his is . . . well . . . playing around. Supposed to nudge the guy in the ribs, wink at him, gee, you son of a gun. But I like you too much to . . ."

"I don't want to hear it," she'd said.

But he'd told her, anyway.

Five years ago.

Tonight, she watched her husband in action at her own dinner table.

A fierce September rain lashed the window panes of their sixth floor apartment, and far below she could hear the sound of automobile tires hissing on wet asphalt. The clock on the dining room wall read exactly ten o'clock. Over coffee and dessert, Bobby was telling a New York atrocity story to their guests. Laura watched him from the opposite end of the long table, listening only distractedly. She knew it was happening again, and that she was helpless to stop it.

Bobby's eyes twinkled as he told the story. He liked New York atrocity stories, especially those about cab drivers. A smile was forming on his mouth now in anticipation of his own punch line. She knew he would burst into immodest laughter the moment he finished the story. She knew him so well. She'd been married to him for nine years. He was her beloved Bobby. Her spouse. Her mate. The father of her two adorable children. Under the table, his left hand was resting on Nessie Winkler's thigh.

"By now, this is the *fifth* time we've circled the Plaza," he said. "Now even if I were fresh off the banana boat, I'd begin to recognize the same hotel going by five *times*, wouldn't you think? I'd begin to maybe *suspect* a little something?"

Had he just squeezed Nessie's thigh under the table?

If not, why had she turned to him in that quick conspiratorial way and looked dopily into his face? Nessie. For Agnes. But you could not call a lissome blonde Agnes. Agnes was for the comic characters of the world. There was nothing funny about Nessie Winkler or the fact that Bobby had his fingers spread on her thigh under the table.

"So finally I tapped on the glass—they're all so terrified of getting held up these days—and he slid open the partition, and I told him he'd better take me to Forty-seventh and Fifth *immediately,* and do you know what he said?"

Lucille came in from the kitchen just then, and stood immediately inside the swinging door, visibly nervous. She was a plain, brown-haired, pudding-faced woman of perhaps twenty-six and Laura suspected this was the first dinner party she'd ever served. Everyone at the table was watching Bobby, waiting to hear the end of his cab-driver story.

Lucille said, "Ma'am?" and Bobby turned to her immediately and snapped, "Would you *mind,* please?"

He leaned toward his guests then, and grinned, and in the heavy Brooklyn accent the cabby must have used, delivered the long-awaited zinger to his story.

"He looked me straight in the eye and said, 'Look, mister, you shoulda *tole* me you was a New Yorker!' "

He burst out laughing, just as Laura knew he would. Nessie burst out laughing, an instant later. Laura laughed, too. Politely. Everyone was laughing but Lucille, who was standing just behind Nessie's chair now, looking somewhat bewildered.

"Yes, Lucille?" Laura said.

"Ma'am, shall I start clearing?"

"Please."

Bobby's hand was still under the table. Laura watched him incredulously. A fork slid off the plate Lucille was lifting from the table, clattering to the floor. She flushed a deep red and immediately knelt beside Nessie's chair to retrieve it. When she rose again, her eyes met Laura's.

117

There was knowledge in those eyes.

She had seen.

"Delicious," Nessie said, and folded her napkin.

At five minutes to twelve, Laura went into the kitchen to pay Mrs. Armstrong and Lucille and to thank them for helping to make the dinner party such a success. Mrs. Armstrong accepted her check and told Laura what a pleasure it always was to work for such a fine lady. Lucille took her check and said nothing. Her eyes avoided Laura's.

Mrs. Armstrong and Lucille were wearing almost identical black topcoats and carrying black handbags. Mrs. Armstrong was carrying a red umbrella. Lucille had no umbrella, and when Laura asked her if she'd like to borrow one, she replied, "No, thank you, ma'am, I'm only catching a bus on Fifth," which was the longest sentence she'd uttered all night long.

Her eyes still avoided Laura's.

It was as if she were somehow blaming Laura for what she'd seen earlier.

When the two women left the apartment, Laura double-locked the service door behind them. Bobby was sprawled on the living room sofa, sipping a cognac and watching an old cowboy movie on television.

"Nice party," he said.

"I thought it went smoothly," Laura said.

"Want a nightcap?"

"Thanks, no. Are the kids okay?"

"What?"

"I asked you to look in on them while I . . ."

"Slipped my mind," Bobby said. "Got involved in the movie here."

"I'll do it," Laura said, and went out of the room and down the corridor to the children's bedrooms.

Both of them were asleep. Seven-year-old Jessica had the blanket twisted around her like a strait jacket, and Laura had difficulty unwinding it without awakening her. She extricated her daughter at last, and then kissed her on the forehead and went next door to where five-year-old Michael was sleeping with his face to the wall. Laura touched his brow, smoothed his hair, kissed him on the cheek, and tucked the blanket tighter around his shoulder.

When she came back into the living room, Bobby was still watching television. He did not look at Laura as she came into the room.

She sat beside him on the sofa and, without preamble, said, "About Nessie."

"What about her?" Bobby asked.

He still did not turn away from the screen, where a band of hapless cowboys were being ambushed at a waterhole by a larger band of Indians.

"Do you find her attractive?" Laura asked. She was not at all asking about Nessie Winkler's attractiveness; only a blind man would not have noticed her startling beauty. She was simply asking whether Bobby was sleeping with her. Nor was she even asking that. She didn't know *what* she was asking. Maybe she only wanted to know if he still loved her.

"I think she's a good-looking woman, yes," Bobby said.

"That doesn't answer my question," Laura said, and became immediately frightened of what might follow. She did not want this confrontation. She had been foolish to bring it to this dangerous point in the short space of several sentences.

Bobby turned from the television screen. His eyes met hers. Blue, steady, level—challenging. Evenly spacing his words, stretching them out interminably, he said, "What, exactly, *is*, your, question?"

119

Tell him, she thought.

Tell him the question is one of trust; you either trust someone completely, or you don't trust him at all.

Tell him you stopped trusting him five years ago.

Tell him you would appreciate it if he kept his whores out of your home where they only embarrass and humiliate you before the hired help.

Tell him, damn it!

"Well?" he said.

She was trembling.

She smiled and said, "I forgot the question."

His eyes held hers a moment longer, as if to make certain the matter had been finally and irrevocably put to rest. He turned back to the television screen.

"I think . . ." Laura started.

"Yes?" he said.

"I think I'll go down for a walk."

"At this hour?"

"I need some air."

"It's still raining, isn't it?"

"I think it's let up."

"Suit yourself," Bobby said, and shrugged.

Laura walked out into the entrance foyer. She took her yellow slicker and rain hat from the closet, put them on, and let herself out of the apartment.

The streets glistened with reflected light, green and yellow and red from the traffic signals, white from the overhead street lamps, a warmer white from the headlights of infrequently passing automobiles. The rain had indeed stopped. The city smelled fresh and clean.

Laura walked.

There was something evocative about the scent of the

streets and the sound of rainwater rushing along the curbs. She could remember coming downstairs after summer thunderstorms when she was a child, taking off her shoes and socks against her mother's wishes, splashing in the curbside puddles. She could remember being fifteen and wildly infatuated with a boy named Charlie, with whom she'd walked dizzily through a springtime city washed by rain. And she could remember meeting Bobby—in the rain.

What do I do now? she wondered.

Do I confront him the way I started to do five minutes ago? What do I say?

Look, Bobby, enough is enough, I want out. I'm thirty-one years old, there's still a life ahead of me if I can find the courage to reach out for it. I don't have to stay married to a man who's got his hands all over every new girl in town, the hell with that.

But is that what I really want to do?

Throw away nine years of marriage because my husband has a few minor flirtations . . . or adventures . . . or affairs . . . or *whatever* the hell you choose to call—damn it, I choose to call them infidelities! He has been *unfaithful* to me!

But . . .

Even so . . .

Do I . . . do I break up a marriage because of infidelity? Even the word sounded old-fashioned. Wouldn't it be better, really, to look the other way, pretend it never happened, pretend it wouldn't happen again?

Like the rainstorm, she thought.

It had been raining at ten o'clock when Bobby explored Nessie's smooth white flesh under a similarly white tablecloth. But the rain had stopped shortly after midnight, and now the streets smelled fresh and clean. There was hardly even a memory of the storm now.

Wasn't that the best way, after all?

Banish each sudden storm to a safe distance in the past, and then quickly forget it?

Bobby was a good provider. The children had a good father. He was handsome, witty, hard-working, and fun to be with most of the time.

Count your blessings, she thought. You've got everything you want or need. He probably loves you to death. It's just that he has a roving eye. It's the same in every marriage. Live with it. Forget it.

The hollow reassurances echoed noisily in her mind, raising a mental clatter so overwhelming that at first she wasn't certain she'd heard the other sound at all. She stopped mid-stride, stood stock still on the sidewalk, heard the click of the traffic signal as the light changed to red at the end of the block.

Silence.

And then the sound again.

A whimper.

She turned toward the brownstone on the right.

The woman lay crouched in the far corner of the small courtyard, in the right angle formed by the facade of the building and the side of the stoop leading to the front door. She was wearing a black coat, and Laura could barely see her until she moved closer to the low iron railing that surrounded the courtyard.

She peered deeper into the gloom.

The woman whimpered again, and Laura went immediately to her. The woman's coat was open, her clothes disarrayed, her dress pulled up over rain-spattered pantyhose.

The pantyhose were jaggedly torn.

At first, they didn't recognize each other.

The courtyard was quite dark, and the woman was

crouched into the deepest corner of it, as if seeking ano-
nymity there. She looked up as Laura knelt beside her, and
flinched as though expecting to be struck. Her eyes were
unfocused, she continued whimpering piteously, and then
the whimper changed to a name, and she repeated the name
over and over again—"Oh, Mrs. Hollis, oh, Mrs. Hollis, oh,
Mrs. Hollis"—as if the litany would invoke the past and
somehow change it to a brighter present. Laura was startled
at first to hear her name, and then she looked into the
woman's face—and saw that it was Lucille.

She leaned in close to her.

Lucille was trying to tell her what had happened. She was
not articulate to begin with, and shock now rendered her
almost unintelligible. Laura gathered that she and Mrs.
Armstrong had parted outside the building, the cook to walk
toward Lexington Avenue to board a subway train, Lucille
toward Fifth to catch a downtown bus. The man had confronted her suddenly . . . stepping out of a doorway . . . ram-
ming his forearm across her throat . . . knife point coming up,
gleaming in the dull glow of the street lamp further up the
street. He'd forced her into the courtyard, into the darkness
. . . forced her legs apart . . . slashed her pantyhose . . .

"I didn't know anybody was on the street with me, I didn't
hear a thing, didn't see a thing until he . . . until he . . ."

Suddenly Lucille was sobbing.

And Laura began to tremble.

She trembled with rage and with fear.

Seeing Lucille this way, vulnerable and exposed, whimpering like a small animal that had been mercilessly beaten,
Laura wanted only to kill whoever had done this, find the
man who had so abused this woman and simply and swiftly
kill him.

At the same time, she was terrified that the man might

suddenly appear again, spring out of the darkness to claim her as his next victim, overpower her as he had Lucille, leave her quaking and whimpering on the stone floor of the same courtyard.

"I'm going to call the police," she said. "If I leave you for a minute, will you be all right?"

"No, please," Lucille said.

"I'm only going as far as the nearest telephone."

"No. I'm bleeding, I think. Oh God, Mrs. Hollis, I'm bleeding."

"The police will send an ambulance."

"No, I don't want the police."

"What?"

"No police. Please."

"Why not?"

"They'll think it was me."

The two women looked at each other, their eyes searching in the darkness.

Somewhere a rainspout poured water into a catch basin. There was the sound of the steady splashing, and then the sharp click of the traffic signal changing again. Their faces were suddenly tinted green.

"I didn't do nothing to cause it," Lucille said.

"I know that."

"The police'll think . . ."

"No, Lucille. They'll think you were victimized."

"No. My husband'll . . ."

"Lucille, we've *got* to call the police."

"No, ma'am, please."

"Did you get a good look at him?"

"Yes."

"Then you've got to describe him to the police."

"No. No, ma'am, please, I can't do that. I can't let my

husband find out about this."

"Lucille . . ."

"Ma'am, if you'll help me find an open drugstore . . ."

"Lucille, listen to me . . ."

"If I can maybe stop the bleeding and get some new panty-hose, then my husband won't know what . . ."

"Your husband's *got* to know, damn it! You were *raped!*" The force of her own voice surprised her.

"He raped you," Laura said.

"I know, ma'am, but . . ."

"You've got to report it to the police."

"Then my husband'll know."

"Yes, Lucille. He'll know you were raped."

"But then he'll think . . ."

"It doesn't matter *what* he thinks. You were a victim, Lucille."

"They won't find him, anyway," Lucille said, shaking her head. "I'll tell them, and they'll know what he looks like, but they won't find him, it won't do any good, they'll think I wanted what happened, they'll . . ."

"*Stop* it!" Laura said.

The courtyard went silent.

Lucille's eyes met Laura's. They were the same eyes that had seen Bobby's hand in Nessie Winkler's lap. They searched Laura's face skeptically now, almost accusingly.

"If it was you," she said, "would *you* go to the police?"

"Yes," Laura said.

Yes, she thought. I would march into a police station and up to the polished brass railing and I would say to the desk sergeant, "I want to report a rape. I've been raped." Yes, she thought. I would.

They continued staring at each other.

Lucille nodded almost imperceptibly.

125

"Yes," Laura said. "Believe me, I would."

Lucille nodded again, more firmly this time.

Laura helped her to her feet and together they walked toward Fifth Avenue in search of a taxi. She had no idea where the local police station was but she expected the cab driver would help them find it. She would stay with Lucille while she talked to the detectives. She would remain by her side and see her through this.

And then she would go back to the apartment where she would hang her yellow slicker and rain hat in the hall closet. And she would go into the bedroom where Bobby would be lying asleep snoring lightly—he always snored so lightly, she knew so much about this man she was now ready to leave.

I want to report a rape, she would say. I've been raped.

A taxi was approaching.

Laura nodded, and then raised her hand to hail it.

But You Know Us

At first, Michael thought it was another false alarm.

But the blips were quite regular.

Pulses at regularly spaced intervals of exactly one second. Precise to one part in a hundred million. And yet . . .

Twenty years ago, Tass reported from the Soviet Union that Gennardy Sholomitsky of the Shternberg Astronomical Institute had detected regularly spaced radio signals that indicated we were not alone in the universe. But the signals had come from a quasar, a starlike object that will emit radio frequency as well as visible radiation. A false alarm, of course. Twelve years ago, the Soviets again intercepted radio signals they thought were of extra-terrestrial origin, signals from a possible Kardashev Type III civilization. A civilization in possession of a transmitting power equal to the energy output of a full galaxy. Tass reported that the signals seemed to be coming from a satellite. Speculated that it was a space probe of the kind visualized by Ronald Bracewell at Stanford. Later admitted, with some embarrassment—

There.

Again.

And again.

He wondered if he should go wake up Lowell.

It had been more than eleven years now since Frank Drake beamed into space—from the radio telescope at Arecibo—his "anti-puzzle," a "code designed to be easily broken." Ever since, listeners all over the world had been waiting for a sign

127

that someone, anyone, had received it and deciphered it. The telescope Michael was monitoring possessed a radio dish capable of scanning nearby galaxies at wavelengths of twenty-one, eighteen, and twelve point six centimeters. Drake's message, in the form of a pictogram using the language of binary arithmetic, first explained how to count from one to ten, then went on to give the atomic numbers for hydrogen, carbon, nitrogen, oxygen and phosphorus, and next gave the components of DNA, the genetic molecule for life on—

The pulses were too regular and too strong to be dismissed.

Michael turned up the gain control.

The screen came into blinding focus, the blip virtually leaping from it.

And simultaneously, the printer alongside the computer monitor began clattering with a jumble of indecipherable glitches and swirls that instantly arranged themselves into what appeared to be Russian and then Chinese characters, and then words unmistakably French, and German, and Spanish and Italian, until finally the single word HELLO appeared in English.

Michael blinked.

The blips had vanished from the screen.

The printer was clattering again.

HELLO, HELLO, HELLO. WE HAVE YOUR MESSAGE. BUT WE DO NOT UNDERSTAND.

He stared at the printer. He thought, Lowell, for God's sake, where are you when I *need* you? He thought, Oh my God, this is . . .

PLEASE RESPOND, YES?

He put his hands on the monitor keyboard.

Hello, he typed cautiously.

The printer began clattering.

YES, HELLO, HELLO, BUT WE HAVE BEEN THROUGH ALL THAT, YES? CENTURIES AGO. WHAT DO YOU WANT?

Michael's hands were trembling on the keyboard. Please say again, he typed. You have received the message? The pictogram?

YES, YES, HELLO. WITH ITS FORMULAS FOR THYMINE, ADENINE, GUANINE AND CYTOSINE, THANK YOU. BUT WE KNOW HOW DNA IS FORMED. YOUR PICTURE OF A HUMAN IS NICE. SO IS THE ONE OF THE RADIO TELESCOPE. AND OF YOUR SOLAR SYSTEM WITH ITS NINE PLANETS. BUT WHAT DO YOU WANT?

Is this a hoax? Michael typed.

A HOAX? NO, NO. A HOAX? NO. POSITIVELY NOT.

Then . . . who . . . what . . . ?

WHAT DO YOU WANT?

Michael began typing furiously. He told whoever it was out there that the space scientists on earth had always wanted *contact,* all they had hoped and prayed for all these years was *contact,* the tiniest signal that could not be attributed to natural radiation emissions, a clear message from space to indicate that the search for extra-terrestrial intelligence had not been in vain. And now this! More than contact! Communication! Actual communication! Over how many light years he could not even hope to guess. Where *are* you? he typed, his fingers racing. *Who* are you?

The printer was silent for a moment.

And then the words formed.

BUT YOU KNOW US.

Michael looked at the printer, certain he had misread the simple sentence. The printer began clattering again.

WE ARE THERE, the words read.

Where? he typed. You are *where?*

ON EARTH.

Here? he typed. But . . .

YOU KNOW US.

Say again, he typed.

YOU KNOW US. WE HAVE BEEN THERE FOR CENTURIES. YOU HAVE BEEN GENEROUS HOSTS.

He blinked at the printer.

WE THANK YOU FOR YOUR HOSPITALITY.

You're welcome, I'm sure, he typed. But . . .

WE LOVE YOU.

But if you've been here for centuries . . .

CENTURIES.

On earth?

YES, CENTURIES.

How can that be possible? he typed. If you're already here, why haven't you made yourselves known to us?

BUT YOU KNOW US.

We *don't* know you, he typed. Please. Who *are* you?

YOU KNOW OUR NAME.

No, we . . .

YOUR NAME FOR US. WE LOVE YOU.

What name? Tell me. Please.

He looked at the printer.

A single word formed.

CANCER.

Running From Legs

Mahogany and brass.

Burnished and polished and gleaming under the green-shaded lights over the bar where men and women alike sat on padded stools and drank. Women, yes. In a saloon, yes, sitting at the bar, and sitting in the black leather booths that lined the dimly lighted room. Women. Drinking alcohol. Discreetly, to be sure, for booze and speakeasies were against the law. Before Prohibition, you rarely saw a woman drinking in a saloon. Now you saw them in speakeasies all over the city. Where once there had been fifteen thousand bars, there were now thirty-two thousand speakeasies. The Prohibitionists hadn't expected these side effects of the Eighteenth Amendment.

The speakeasy was called the Brothers Three, named after Bruno Tataglia and his brothers Angelo and Mickey. It was located just off Third Avenue on 87th Street, in a part of the city named Yorkville after the Duke of York. We were here celebrating. My grandmother owned a chain of lingerie shops she called "Scanties," and today had been the grand opening of the third one. Her boyfriend Vinnie was with us, and so was Dominique Lefevre, who worked for her in the second of her shops, the one on Lexington Avenue. My parents would have been here, too, but they'd been killed in an automobile accident while I was overseas.

In the other room, the band was playing "Ja-Da," a tune from the war years. We were all drinking from coffee cups. In the coffee cups was something very brown and very vile tasting, but it was not coffee.

Dominique was smiling.

It occurred to me that perhaps she was smiling at me.

Dominique was twenty-eight years old, a beautiful, dark-haired, dark-eyed woman, tall and slender and utterly desirable. A native of France, she had come to America as a widow shortly after the war ended; her husband had been killed three days before the guns went silent. One day, alone with her in my grandmother's shop—Dominique was folding silk panties, I was sitting on a stool in front of the counter, watching her—she told me she despaired of ever finding another man as wonderful as her husband had been. "I 'ave been spoil', *n'est-ce pas?*" she said. I adored her French accent. I told her that I, too, had suffered losses in my life. And so, like cautious strangers fearful of allowing even our *glances* to meet, we'd skirted the possibilities inherent in our chance proximity.

But now—her smile.

The Brothers Three was very crowded tonight. Lots of smoke and laughter and the sound of a four-piece band coming from the other room. Piano, drums, alto saxophone, and trumpet. There was a dance floor in the other room. I wondered if I should ask Dominique to dance. I had never danced with her. I tried to remember when last I'd danced with anyone.

I'd been limping, yes. And a French girl whispered in my ear—this was after I'd got out of the hospital, it was shortly after the armistice was signed—a French girl whispered to me in Paris that she found a man with a slight limp very sexy. "*Je trouve tres seduisante,*" she said, "*une claudication legere.*" She had nice *poitrines*, but I'm not sure I believed her. I think she was just being kind to an American doughboy who'd got shot in the foot during the fighting around the Bois des Loges on a bad day in November. I found that somewhat humiliating, getting shot in the foot. It did not seem very heroic, getting shot in the foot. I no longer limped, but I still had the feeling that some people thought I'd shot *myself* in the goddamn foot. To get out of the 78th Division or something. As if such a thought had ever crossed my mind.

Dominique kept smiling at me.

Boozily.

I figured she'd had too much coffee.

She was wearing basic black tonight. A simple black satin, narrow in silhouette, bare of back, its neckline square and adorned with pearls, its waistline low, its hemline falling to mid-thigh where a three-inch expanse of white flesh separated the dress from the rolled tops of her blond silk stockings. She was smoking. As were Vinnie and my grandmother. Smoking had something to do with drinking. If you drank, you smoked. That seemed to be the way it worked.

Dominique kept drinking and smoking and smiling at me.

I smiled back.

My grandmother ordered another round.

She was drinking Manhattans. Dominique was drinking Martinis. Vinnie was drinking something called a Between the Sheets, which was one-third brandy, one-third Cointreau, one-third rum, and a dash of lemon juice. I was drinking a Bosom Caresser. These were all cocktails, an American word made popular when drinking became illegal. Cocktails.

In the other room, a double paradiddle and a solid bass drum shot ended the song. There was a pattering of applause, a slight expectant pause, and then the alto saxophone soared into the opening riff of a slow, sad, and bluesy rendition of "Who's Sorry Now?"

133

"Richard?" Dominique said, and raised one eyebrow. "Aren't you going to ask me to dance?"

She was easily the most beautiful woman in the room. Eyes lined with black mascara, lips and cheeks painted the color of all those poppies I'd seen growing in fields across the length and breadth of France. Her dark hair bobbed in a shingle cut, the scent of mimosa wafting across the table.

"Richard?"

Her voice a caress.

Alto saxophone calling mournfully from the next room.

Smoke swirling like fog coming in off the docks on the day we landed over there. We were back now because it was *over* over there. And I no longer limped. And Dominique was asking me to dance.

"Go dance with her," my grandmother said.

"Yes, come," Dominique said, and put out her cigarette. Rising, she moved out of the booth past my grandmother, who rescued her Manhattan by holding it close to her protective bosom, and then winked at me as if to say "These are new times, Richie, we have the vote now, we can drink and we can smoke, anything goes nowadays, Richie. Go dance with Dominique."

Is what my grandmother's wink seemed to say.

I took Dominique's hand.

Together, hand in hand, we moved toward the other room.

"I love this song," Dominique said, and squeezed my hand.

There were round tables with white tablecloths in the other room, embracing a half-moon-shaped, highly polished, parquet dance floor. The lights were dimmer in this part of the club, perhaps because the foxtrot was a new dance that encouraged cheeks against cheeks and hands upon asses. A party of three—a handsome man in a dinner jacket and two women in gowns—sat at one of the tables with Bruno Tataglia. Bruno was leaning over the table, in obviously obsequious conversation with the good-looking man whose eyes kept checking out women on the dance floor even though there was one beautiful woman sitting on his left and another on his right. Both women were wearing white satin gowns and they both had purple hair. I had heard of women wearing orange, or red, or green, or even purple wigs when they went out on the town, but this was the first time I'd ever actually *seen* one.

Two, in fact.

I wondered how Dominique would look in a purple wig.

"Dominique?"

Bruno's voice.

He rose as we came abreast of the table, took her elbow, and said to the man in the dinner jacket, "Mr. Noland, I'd like you to meet the beauteous Dominique."

"Pleasure," Mr. Noland said.

Dominique nodded politely.

"And Richie here," Bruno said as an afterthought.

"Nice to meet you," I said.

Mr. Noland's eyes were on Dominique.

"Won't you join us?" he said.

"Thank you, but we're about to dance," Dominique said, and squeezed my hand again, and led me out onto the floor. I held her close. We began swaying in time to the music. The trumpet player was putting in a mute. The piano player eased him into his solo.

Liquid brass.

Dominique's left hand moved up to the back of my neck.

"You dance well," she said.

"Thank you."

135

"Does it ever ache you? Your foot?"

"When it rains," I said.

"Was it terrible, the war?" she asked.

"Yes," I said.

I did not much feel like talking about it. I gently steered her away from the ring of tables and back toward the bandstand, sweeping her gracefully past the table where Bruno was grinning oleaginously at Mr. Noland and his two blond bimbos.

Mr. Noland's eyes met mine.

A shiver ran up my spine.

I had never seen eyes like that in my life.

Not even on the battlefield.

Not even on men eager to kill me.

Dominique and I glided over the parquet floor.

Drifting, drifting to the sound of the muted horn.

There was a gentle tap on my shoulder.

I turned.

Mr. Noland was standing slightly behind me and slightly to my right, his hand resting on my shoulder.

"I'm cutting in," he said.

And his hand tightened on my shoulder, and he moved me away from Dominique, my left hand still holding her right hand, and then stepped into the open circle his intrusion had created, looping his right arm around Dominique's waist and shouldering me out completely.

I moved clumsily off the dance floor and stood in the middle of the arch separating the two rooms, feeling somehow embarrassed and inadequate, watching helplessly as Mr. Noland pulled Dominique in close to him. At the table he'd just vacated, the two women were laughing it up with Bruno. I went through the arch and back into the lounge with its black leather booths and its black leather barstools. My grandmother raised her Manhattan to me in a toast. I nodded acknowledgment, and smiled, and walked toward where Mickey Tataglia was sitting at the bar, chatting up a redhead, who was wearing a windblown bob and a liquid green dress the color of her eyes. He had his hand on her silk-stockinged knee. She had in her hand, I swear to God, a long cigarette holder that made her look exactly like any of the Held flappers on the covers of *Life*. This was a night for firsts. I had never seen two women with purple wigs, and I had never seen a woman with a cigarette holder like this one. I had never danced with Dominique either; easy come, easy go.

As I took the stool on his left, Mickey was telling the redhead all about his war experiences. His brother Angelo was behind the bar, filling coffee cups with booze. I told him I wanted a Bosom Caresser.

"What's a Bosom Caresser?" he asked.

"I have no idea," I said. "Our waiter asked me if I wanted one, and I said yes, and he brought it to me."

"What's in it?"

"Mickey," I said, "what's in a Bosom Caresser?"

"Talk about *fresh!*" the redhead said, and rolled her eyes.

"Are you asking what I would *put* in a Bosom Caresser?" Mickey said. "If I were making such a drink?"

"Who is this person you're talking to?" the redhead said.

"A friend of mine," Mickey said. "This is Maxie," he said, and squeezed her knee.

"How do you do?" I said.

"This is Richie," he said.

"Familiar for Richard," I said.

"I'm familiar for Maxine," Maxie said.

In the other room, the band started playing "Mexicali Rose."

"If you want a Bosom Treasure, you got to tell me

what's in it," Angelo said.

"Bosom *Caresser*," I said.

"Whatever," Angelo said. "I have to know the ingredients."

"Mother's milk, to begin with," Mickey said.

"You're as fresh as he is," Maxie scolded, rolling her eyes at me and playfully slapping Mickey's hand, which was working higher on her knee.

"Laced with gin and egg white," I said.

"Ick," Maxie said.

"And topped with a cherry," Mickey said.

"*Double*-ick," Maxie said.

"We don't have any mother's milk," Angelo said.

"Then I'll have a Rock 'n' Rye," I said.

"I'll have another one of these, whatever it is," Mickey said.

"Ditto," Maxie said.

"Hold the fort," Mickey said, getting off his stool. "I have to visit the gents."

I watched him as he headed toward the men's room. He stopped at my grandmother's table, planted a noisy kiss on her cheek, and then moved on.

"Was he really a war hero?" Maxie asked me.

"Oh, sure," I said. "He was in the battle of—"

"Just keep your damn hands *off* me!" Dominique shouted from the dance floor.

I was off that stool as if I'd heard an incoming artillery shell whistling toward my head. Off that stool and running toward the silvered arch beyond which were the tables with their white tablecloths and the polished parquet dance floor, and Dominique in her short black dress, trying to free her right hand from—

"Let *go* of me!" she shouted.

"No."

A smile on Mr. Noland's face. His hand clutched around her narrow waist.

Maybe he didn't see her eyes. Maybe he was too busy getting a big charge out of this slender, gorgeous woman trying to extricate herself from his powerful grip.

"Damn you!" she said. "Let go or I'll . . ."

"Yes, baby, what is it you'll do?"

She didn't tell him what she'd do. She simply did it. She twisted her body to the left, her arm swinging all the way back and then forward again with all the power of her shoulder behind it. Her bunched left fist collided with Mr. Noland's right cheek, just below his eye, and he touched his eye, and looked at his fingertips as if expecting blood, and then very softly and menacingly said, "Now you get hurt, baby."

Some people never learn.

He had called her "baby" once, and that had been a bad mistake, so what he'd just done was call her "baby" again, which was an even bigger mistake. Dominique nodded curtly, the nod saying "Okay, fine," and then she went for his face with both hands, her nails raking bloody tracks from just under his eyes—which I think she'd been going for—all the way down to his jawline.

Mr. Noland punched her.

Hard.

I yelled the way I'd yelled going across the Marne.

I was on him in ten seconds flat, the time it took to race through that arch and charge across the dance floor, the time it took to clench my fists and hit him first with the left one and then with the right one, bam-bam, a one-two punch to the gut and the jaw that sent him staggering back from me. He rubbed his jaw in surprise. His hands came away with the blood from Dominique's fingernail-raking. He looked at the

139

blood in surprise too. And then he looked at me in surprise, as if trying to figure out how some madman had got inside this civilized speakeasy. He didn't say a word. He merely looked surprised and sad and bloody, shaking his head as if wondering how the world had turned so rotten all at once. And then, abruptly, he stopped shaking his head and took a gun out of a holster under his dinner jacket.

Just like that.

Zip.

One minute, no gun. The next minute, a gun.

Dominique took off one of her high-heeled shoes.

As she raised her leg, Mr. Noland looked under her skirt at her underwear—black silk panties in my grandmother's "sirocco" line, $4.98 over the counter in any of her shops. Mr. Noland then realized what Dominique was going to do with the shoe. What she was going to do was hit him on the other side of the head with it. Which was possibly why he aimed the gun right at her heart.

I did the only thing I could do.

In reaction, Mr. Noland bellowed in rage and doubled over in pain, his hands clutching for his groin, his knees coming together as if he had to pee very badly, and then he fell to the floor and lay there writhing and moaning while everywhere about him were dancers all aghast. Bruno rushed to him at once and knelt beside him, his hands fluttering. "Oh, God, Mr. Noland," he said, "I'm so sorry, Mr. Noland," and Mr. Noland tried to say something but his face was very red and his eyes were bulging and all that came out was a sort of strangled sputter at which point one of the women with the purple hair came running over and said, "Legs? Shall I call a doctor?"

Which is when I grabbed Dominique's hand and began running.

★ ★ ★ ★ ★

"A bootlegger, a narcotics smuggler, a hijacker, and a trusted friend of an even *bigger* gangster named Little Augie Orgen, *that's* who Legs *Diamond* is."

All this from Mickey Tataglia, who hurried us through tunnels under the club, pressing buttons that opened doors into other tunnels lined with booze smuggled in from Canada.

"He also owns a second-floor speakeasy called the Hotsy Totsy Club on Broadway, between Fifty-fourth and Fifty-fifth streets, that's who Legs Diamond is. You did a stupid thing, both of you. Do you know who arranged the murder of Jack the Dropper?"

"Who is Jack the Dropper?" Dominique asked.

High heels clicking, long legs flashing through dusty underground tunnels lined with cases and cases of illegal booze. Mickey walked swiftly ahead of us, leading the way, brushing aside cobwebs that hung from rafters along which rats scampered.

"Jack the Dropper," he said impatiently. "Alias Kid Dropper, whose real name is Nathan Kaplan, who all three of him was shot dead by Louis Kushner in a trap the Diamonds set up."

"The Diamonds," I said.

"Legs Diamond," Mickey said. "Alias Jack Diamond, alias John Higgins, alias John Hart, whose real name is John Thomas *Noland,* who all five of him will not like getting kicked in the balls by a fucking dope who shot himself in the foot."

"Richard did not shoot himself in the foot," Dominique said heatedly.

"I'm sure the Diamonds will take that into consideration when he kills you both. Or if not him, then one of his apes.

141

The Diamonds has a lot of such people on his payroll. I wish you both a lot of luck," he said, and pressed another button. A wall swung open. Beyond it was an alleyway.

"You're on 88th Street," Mickey said.

We stepped outside into a dusky evengloam.

Mickey hit the button again.

The door closed behind us.

We began running.

We got to Penn Station at 8:33 P.M. and learned that a train would be leaving for Chattanooga, Tennessee, in exactly seven minutes. It cost us an additional twelve dollars each for a sleeping compartment, but we figured it was worth it. We did not want to be sitting out in the open should any of Diamond's goons decide to check out the trains leaving the city. A sleeping compartment had windows with curtains and shades on them. A sleeping compartment had a door with a lock on it.

The train was the Crescent Limited, making stops in Philadelphia, Baltimore, Washington, D.C., Charlottesville, Spartanburg, Greenville, and Atlanta, before its scheduled arrival in Chattanooga at 10:10 tomorrow night. We figured Chattanooga was far enough away. The total one-way fare came to $41.29 for each of us. The train was scheduled to leave at 8:40.

A black porter carried our bags into the compartment, told us he'd make up the berths for us whenever we liked, and then inquired as to whether we'd care for any kind of beverage before we retired.

The "any kind of beverage" sounded like a code, but I wanted to make certain.

"What kind of beverage did you have in mind?" I asked.

"Whatever sort of beverage might suit your fancy," he said.

"And what sort of beverage might that be?"

"Well, suh," he said, "we has coffee, tea, and milk . . ."

"Uh-huh."

"And a *wide* variety of soft drinks," he said, and winked so broadly that any Prohibition agent wandering past would have arrested him on the strength of the wink alone. Dominique immediately pulled back her skirt, took a silver flask from where it was tucked into her garter, and asked the porter to fill it with any kind of colorless soft drink, please. I took my flask from my hip pocket and told him I'd have the same. He knew we both wanted gin. Or its vague equivalent.

"That'll be twenty dollars each t'fill dese flasks here," he said.

"We'll need some setups too," I said, and took out my wallet and handed him three twenty-dollar bills. He left the compartment and returned some ten minutes later, carrying a tray on which were a siphon bottle of soda, two tall glasses, a bowl of chipped ice with a spoon in it, a lemon on a small dish, a paring knife, and ten dollars in change from the sixty I'd given him. He put the tray on the table between the two facing seats, removed the two filled flasks from the side pockets of his white jacket, put those on the table as well, asked if there was anything else we might be needing, and then told us again that he would make up the berths for us whenever we were of a mind to retire. Dominique said maybe he ought to make them up now. I looked at her.

"No?" she said.

"No, fine," I said.

"Shall I makes 'em up, den?" the porter asked.

"Please," Dominique said.

The porter grinned; I suspected he wanted to get the bed-making over with so he could get a good night's sleep himself. We went out into the corridor, leaving him to his work. Dominique looked at her watch.

I looked at my watch.

It was already ten minutes to nine.

"I'm very frightened," she said.

"So am I."

"You?" She waved this away with the back of her hand. "You have been in the war."

"Still," I said, and shrugged.

She did not know about wars.

Inside the compartment, the porter worked in silence.

"Why aren't we leaving yet?" Dominique asked.

I looked at my watch again.

"There you go, suh," the porter said, stepping out into the corridor.

"Thank you," I said, and tipped him two dollars.

" 'Night, suh," he said, touching the peak of his hat, "ma'am, sleep well, the boths of you."

We went back into the compartment. He had left the folding table up because he knew we'd be drinking, but the seats on either side of the compartment were now made up as narrow beds with pillows and sheets and blankets. I closed and locked the door behind us.

"Did you lock it?" Dominique asked. She was already spooning ice into both glasses, her back to me.

"I locked it," I said.

"Tell me how much," she said, and began pouring from one of the flasks.

"That's enough," I said.

"I want a very strong one," she said, pouring heavily into the other glass.

"Shall I slice this lemon?"

"Please," she said, and sat on the bed on the forward side of the compartment.

I sat opposite her. She picked up the soda siphon, squirted some into each of the glasses. Her legs were slightly parted. Her skirt was riding high on her thighs. Rolled silk stockings. Garter on her right leg, where the flask had been. I halved the lemon, quartered it, squeezed some juice into her glass, dropped the crushed quarter-lemon into it. I raised my own glass.

"Pas de citron pour toi?" she asked.

"I don't like lemon."

"It will taste vile without lemon," she said.

"I don't want to spoil the flavor of premium gin," I said.

Dominique laughed.

"A votre santé," I said, and clinked my glass against hers.

We both drank.

It went down like molten fire.

"Jesus!" I said.

"Whoooo!" she said.

"I think I'm going blind!"

"That is not something to joke about."

The train began huffing and puffing.

"Are we leaving?" she asked.

"Enfin," I said.

"Enfin, d'accord," she said, and heaved a sigh of relief.

The train began moving. I thought of the train that had taken us from Calais to the front.

"Now we can relax," she said.

I nodded.

"Do you think he'll send someone after us?"

"Depends on how crazy he is."

"I think he is very crazy."

"So do I."

"Then he will send someone."

"Maybe."

145

Dominique drew back the curtains on the outside window, lifted the shade. We were out of the tunnel now, already into the night. There were stars overhead. No moon.

"Best to just *sip* this stuff," I said. "Otherwise . . ."

"Ah, oui, bien sûr," she said.

We sipped at the gin. The train was moving along swiftly now, flashing southward into the night.

"So you learned some French over there," she said.

"A little."

"Well . . . *a votre santé* . . . *enfin* . . . quite a bit of French, no?"

"Only enough to get by on."

I was thinking of the German who had mistaken us for French troops and who'd pleaded with us in broken French to spare his life. I was thinking of his skull exploding when our patrol sergeant opened fire.

"This grows on you, doesn't it?" I said.

"Actually, I think it's very good," she said. "I think it may even be real gin."

"Maybe," I said dubiously.

She looked over her glass at me. "Maybe next time there's a war, you won't have to go," she said.

"Because I was wounded, do you mean?"

"Yes."

"Maybe."

The train raced through the night. The New Jersey countryside flashed by in the darkness. Telephone wires swooped and dipped between poles.

"They say there are thirty telephone poles to every mile," I said.

"Vraiment?"

"Well, that's what they say."

"Turn off the lights," she said. "It will look prettier outside."

I turned off the lights.

"And open the window, please. It will be cooler."

I tried pulling up one of the windows, but it wouldn't budge. I finally got the other one up. Cool air rushed into the compartment. There was the smell of smoke from the engine up ahead, cinders and soot on the night.

"Ahhh, yes," she said, and sighed deeply.

Outside, the world rushed past.

We sat sipping the gin, watching the distant lights.

"Do you think Mr. Diamonds will have us killed?"

"Mr. *Diamond*," I said. "Singular. Legs Diamond."

"I wonder why they call him Legs."

"I don't know."

She fell silent. Staring through the window. Face in profile. Touched only by starshine.

"I love the sound of the wheels," she said, and sighed again. "Trains are so sad."

I was thinking the very same thing.

"I'm getting sleepy, are you?" she asked.

"A little."

"I think I'll get ready for bed."

"I'll step outside," I said, and started to get up.

"No, stay," she said, and then, "It's dark."

She rose, reached up to the overhead rack, and took down her suitcase. She snapped open the locks, and lifted the lid. She reached behind her, then, and unbuttoned the buttons at the back of her dress and pulled the dress up over her head.

I turned away, toward the windows.

We were coming through a stretch of farmland, lights only in the far distance now, nothing close to the tracks. The single closed window reflected Dominique in black lingerie from

147

my grandmother's "Flirty Flapper" line, rolled black seamed silk stockings, black lace-edged bra designed to flatten her breasts, black lace-edged tap pants.

The blackness of the night reflected her.

"Pour me some more gin, please," she said. Softly.

I spooned ice into her glass, unscrewed the flask's top, poured gin over the ice. Silver spilled from silver onto silver. Behind me, there was the rustle of silk.

"A little lemon, please," she said.

In the reflecting window, she was naked now. Pale as starlight.

She took a nightgown out of the suitcase.

I squeezed another quarter-lemon, dropped it into the glass. I squirted soda into the glass. She dropped the nightgown over her head. It slid down past her breasts and hips and thighs.

I turned to her, she turned to me. In the nightgown, she looked almost medieval. The gown was either silk or rayon, as white as snow, its yoke neck trimmed with white lace. My grandmother's "Sleeptite" line.

I handed Dominique her drink.

"Thank you," she said, and looked at my empty glass on the table. "None for you?" she asked.

"I think I've had enough."

"Just a sip," she said. "To drink a toast. I can't drink a toast all alone."

I dropped some ice into my glass, poured a little gin over it.

She raised her glass.

"To now," she said.

"There's no such thing," I said.

"Tonight, then. There is surely tonight."

"Yes. I suppose."

"Will you drink to tonight, then?"

"To tonight," I said.

"And to us."

I looked at her.

"To us, Richard."

"To us," I said.

We drank.

"Doesn't this table move out of the way?" she asked.

"I think it folds down," I said.

"Can you fold it down?"

"If you like."

"Well, I think it's in the way, don't you?"

"I guess it is."

"Well, then, please fold it down, Richard."

I moved everything from the table to the wide sill just inside the window. I got on my knees then, looked under the table, figured out how the hinge and clasp mechanism worked, and lowered the top.

"*Voilà!*" Dominique said triumphantly.

I picked up my drink from the windowsill. We both sat, Dominique on one bed, I on the other, facing each other, our knees almost touching. Outside, the countryside rolled by, an occasional light splintering the dark.

"I wish we had music," she said. "We could dance again. There's enough room for dancing now, don't you think? With the table down?"

I looked at her skeptically; the space between the beds was perhaps three feet wide by six feet long.

"Without being interrupted this time," she said, and tossed her head and began swaying from side to side.

"I shouldn't have let him cut in," I said.

"Well, how could you have known?"

"I saw his eyes."

"Behind you? When he was cutting in?"

"Earlier. I should have known. Seeing those eyes."

"Dance with me now," she said, and held out her arms.

"We don't have music," I said.

She moved in close against me.

The soft silken feel of her.

"Ja-Da," she sang.

Slowly.

Very slowly.

"Ja-Da . . ."

Not at all in the proper tempo.

"Ja-Da, Ja-Da . . .

"Jing . . . jing . . . *jing.*"

I thought at first . . .

"Ja-Da . . ."

What I thought . . .

"Ja-Da . . ."

Was that . . .

"Ja-Da, Ja-Da . . ."

Was that a fierce thrust of her crotch accompanied each . . .

"Jing . . . jing . . . *jing.*"

I was flamingly erect in the tick of an instant.

"Oh, *mon Dieu,*" Dominique whispered.

Whispered those words in that rumbling sleeping compartment, on that train hurtling through the night, speeding us southward and away from all possible harm, lurching through the darkness, causing us to lose our balance so that we fell still locked in embrace onto the bed that was Dominique's, holding her tight in my arms, kissing her forehead and her cheeks and her nose and her lips and her neck and her shoulders and her breasts as she whispered over and over again, "Oh, *mon Dieu,* oh, *mon Dieu,* oh *mon Dieu.*"

We brought to the act of love a steamy clumsiness composed of legs and arms and hips and noses and chins in constant collision. The train, the track, seemed maliciously intent on hurling us out of bed and out of embrace. We jostled and jiggled on that thin mattress, juggling passion, sweating in each other's arms as we struggled to maintain purchase. "Ow!" she said as my elbow poked her in the ribs. "Sorry," I mumbled, and then "Ooops!" because I was sliding out of her. She adjusted her hips, lifting them, deeply enclosing me again but almost knocking me off her in the bargain because the train in that very instant decided to run over an imperfection on the track which together with the motion of her ascending hips sent me soaring ceilingward. The only thing that kept me in her and on her was the cunning interlocking design of our separate parts.

We learned quickly enough.

Although, in retrospect, the train did all the work and we were merely willing accomplices.

Up and down the train went, rocketing through the night, in and out of tunnels the train went, rocketing through the night, side to side the train rocked, rattling through the night, up and down, in and out, side to side, the train thrust against the night, tottering the darkness with a single searing eye, scattering all before it helter-skelter. Helpless in the grip of this relentless fucking machine, we screamed at last aloud and together, waking the hall porter in the corridor, who screamed himself as though he'd heard shrieks of bloody murder.

And then we lay enfolded in each other's arms and talked. We scarcely knew each other, except intimately, and had never really talked seriously. So now we talked about things, that were enormously important to us. Like our favorite colors. Or our favorite times of the year. Or our favorite ice-cream flavors. Or our favorite songs and movies. Our dreams. Our ambitions.

I told her I loved her.

I told her I would do anything in the world for her.

"Would you kill someone for me?" she asked.

"Yes," I said at once.

She nodded.

"I knew you were watching me undress," she said. "I knew you were looking at my reflection in the window. I found that very exciting."

"So did I."

"And getting bounced all around while you were inside me, that was very exciting too."

"Yes."

"I wish you were inside me now," she said.

"Yes."

"Bouncing around inside me."

"Yes."

"That big thing inside me again," she said, and leaned over me and kissed me on the mouth.

Vinnie had bad news when I called home that Saturday.

On Friday afternoon, while Dominique and I were on the train heading south, two men accosted my grandmother as she came out of her Fourteenth Street shop.

"In the car, Grandma," the skinny one said.

He was the one with the crazy eyes.

That's the way my grandmother later described him to Vinnie.

"He had crazy eyes," she said. "And a knife."

The fat one was behind the wheel of the car. My grandmother described the car as a two-door blue Jewett coach. All three of them sat up front. The fat one driving, my grandmother in the middle, and the skinny one on her right. What the skinny one did, he put the knife under her chin and told her if You-Know-Who did not come back to face the music, the next time he would be looking in at her tonsils, did she catch his drift?

My grandmother caught his drift, all right.

They let her out of the car on Avenue B and East Fourth Street, right near the Most Holy Redeemer Catholic Church. She ran in terror all the way home. Vinnie grabbed a baseball bat and went looking for Fat and Skinny in the streets. He could not find them, nor did he see a single Jewett coach anywhere in the entire 9th Precinct.

"So what do you think?" he asked me on the phone.

"I think I'll have to kill him," I said.

"Who?"

"Legs Diamond."

There was a long silence.

"Vinnie," I said, "did you hear me?"

"I heard you," he said. "I don't think that's such a good idea, Richie."

The wires between us crackled; we were a long way away from each other.

"Vinnie," I said, "I can't hide from this man forever."

"He'll grow tired of hounding you," he said.

"No, I don't think so. He has a lot of people who can do the hounding for him. It's no trouble at all for him, really."

"Richie, listen to me."

"Yes, Vinnie, I'm listening."

"What do you want from life, Richie?"

"I want to marry Dominique," I said. "And I want to have children with her."

"Ah," he said.

"And I want to live in a house with a white picket fence around it."

"Yes," he said. "And that's why you mustn't kill this man."

"No," I said, "that's why I *must* kill this man. Because otherwise . . ."

"Richie, it's not easy to kill someone."

"I've seen a lot of people killing a lot of people, Vinnie. It looked easy to me."

"In a war, yes. But unless you're in a war, it's not so easy to kill someone. Have you ever killed anyone, Richie?"

"No."

"In a war, it's easy," he said. "Everyone is shooting at everyone else, so if *your* bullet doesn't happen to kill anyone, it doesn't matter. Someone *else's* bullet will. But killing somebody in a war isn't *murder,* Richie. That's the first thing a soldier learns; killing someone in a war isn't murder. Because when everyone is killing someone, then *no* one is *killing* anyone."

"Well . . ."

"Don't 'well' me, just listen to me. Killing Legs Diamond will be murder. Are you ready to do murder, Richie?"

"Yes," I said.

"Why?"

"Because I love Dominique. And if I don't kill him, he'll hurt her."

"Look . . . let me ask around, okay?" Vinnie said.

"Ask around?"

"Here and there. Meanwhile, don't do anything foolish."

"Vinnie?" I said. "I know where he is. It's in all the newspapers."

I heard a sigh on the other end of the line.

"He's in Troy, New York. They're putting him on trial for kidnapping some kid up there."

"Richie . . ."

"I think I'd better go up to Troy, Vinnie."

"No, Richie," he said. "Don't."

There was another long silence on the line.

"I didn't think it would end this way, Vinnie," I said.

"It doesn't have to end this way."

"I thought . . ."

"What did you think, Richie?"

"I never thought it would get down to killing him. Running from him was one thing, but killing him . . ."

"It doesn't have to get down to that," Vinnie said.

"It does," I said. "It does."

Five hours and thirty-one minutes after the jury began deliberating the case, Legs Diamond was found innocent of all charges against him.

When he and his entourage came out of the courthouse that night, Dominique and I were waiting in a car parked across the street. We were both dressed identically. Long black men's overcoats, black gloves, pearl-gray fedoras.

It was bitterly cold.

Diamond and his family got into a taxi he had hired to chauffeur him to and from the courthouse during the trial. The rest of his party got into cars behind him. In our own car, a maroon sedan, Dominique and I followed them into Albany and then to a speakeasy at 518 Broadway. We did not go into the club. We sat in the car and waited. We did not talk at all. It was even colder now. The windows became rimed with frost. I kept rubbing at the windshield with my gloved hand.

At a little after one in the morning, Diamond and his wife Alice came out of the club. Diamond was wearing a brown chinchilla coat and a brown fedora. Alice was wearing a dress, high-heeled shoes, no coat. The driver came out of the club a moment later. From where we were parked, we could not hear the conversation between Alice and Diamond, but as he walked with his driver toward where the taxi was parked, he yelled over his shoulder, "Stick around till I get back!" The driver got in behind the wheel. Diamond climbed into the backseat. Alice stood on the sidewalk a moment longer, plumes of vapor trailing from her mouth, and then went back into the club. We gave the taxi a reasonable lead and then pulled out after them.

The taxi took Diamond to a rooming house on the corner of Clinton Avenue and Tenbroeck Street. Diamond got out, said something to the driver, closed the door, and went into the building. We drove past, turned the corner, went completely around the block, and then parked halfway up the street. The cab was still parked right in front of the building. We could not have got by the driver without being seen.

Diamond came out at 4:30 A.M.

I nudged Dominique awake.

We began following the taxi again.

Ten days ago, a man and a woman named "Mr. and Mrs. Kelly" had rented three rooms in a rooming house on Dove Street—for themselves and their relatives, a sister-in-law and her ten-year-old son. I learned this from the owner of the rooming house, a woman named Laura Wood, who gave me the information after she identified some newspaper photographs I showed her. She seemed surprised that Mr. Kelly was in fact the big gangster Legs Diamond who was being tried "over in Troy." She told me he was a respectable gentleman, quiet and well behaved, and she had no real cause for complaint. I gave her fifty dollars and asked her not to mention that a reporter had been there.

The taxi took Diamond there now.

Sixty-seven Dove Street.

Diamond got out of the taxi. It was a quarter to five in the morning. The taxi drove off. The street was silent. Not a light showed in the rooming house. He unlocked the front door with a key, and went inside. The door closed behind him. The street was silent again. We waited. On the second floor of the rooming house, a light came on.

"Do you think the wife is already here?" Dominique asked.

"He told her to stay at the club."

"What will you do if she's there with him?"

"I don't know," I said.

"You will have to kill her, too, no?"

"First let me get in the building, okay?"

"No, I want to know."

"What is it you want to know?"

"What you will do if she is there with him."

"I'll see."

"Well, I think you will have to kill her, no?"

"Dominique, there is killing and there is killing."

"Yes, I know that. But if you go in there, you must be prepared to do what must be done. Otherwise, his people will come after us again and again. You know that."

"Yes. I know that."

"We will have to keep running."

"I know."

"So if the woman is there with him, you will have to kill her, too. That is only logical, Richard. You cannot leave her alive to identify you."

I nodded.

"If she is there, you must kill them both, it is as simple as that. If you love me."

"I do love you."

"And I love you," she said.

The light on the second floor went out.

"Bonne chance," she said, and kissed me on the mouth.

I left her sitting behind the wheel of the car, its engine running.

I tried the front door of the rooming house.

Locked.

I leaned hard on the door. The lock seemed almost ready to give. I backed away, lifted my left leg, and kicked at the door flat-footed, just above the knob. The lock snapped, the door sprang inward.

Silently, I climbed the steps to the second floor. Mrs. Wood had innocently told me that Diamond and his wife were staying in the room on the right of the stairway. "Such a quiet couple," she'd said. The steps creaked under me as I went up. A nightlight was burning on the second floor. Almost too dim to see by. A shabby carpet underfoot. I turned to the right. The door to Diamond's room was at the end of the hall. I took a gun from each pocket of my overcoat. I had loaded both pistols with softnosed bullets. Dum-dums. If I was going to do this, it had to be done right.

I tried the doorknob.

The door was unlocked.

I eased it open.

The room was dark except for the faintest glow of daybreak beyond the drawn window shade. I could hear Diamond's shallow breathing across the room. A leather traveling bag was on the floor. His chinchilla coat lay beside it. So did his hat. His trousers were folded over the back of a chair. I went to the bed. I looked down at him. He was sleeping with his mouth open. He stank of booze. My hands were trembling.

My first bullet went into the wall.

The next one went into the floor.

I finally shot Diamond in the head three times.

I came tearing down the steps. The front door was still ajar. I ran out into a cold gray dawn. A man coming out of the building next door saw me racing across the street to where Dominique was standing outside the car on the passenger side, the engine idling, the exhaust throwing up gray clouds on the gray dawn.

"Was she there?" she asked.

"No," I said.

"Did you kill him?"

"Yes."

"Good."

Across the street, the man was staring at us.

We got into the car and began driving north. I was behind the wheel now. Dominique was wiping the guns. Just in case. Wiping, wiping with a white silk handkerchief, polishing those gun butts and barrels in the event that somehow, in spite of the gloves, I'd left fingerprints on them. As we approached St. Paul's Church, a mile and a half from Dove Street, I slowed the car. Dominique rolled down the window on her side, and threw out one of the guns, wrapped in the silk handkerchief. Five minutes later, she tossed out the second gun, wrapped in another handkerchief. We sped through dawn. In Saugerties, a uniformed policeman looked up in surprise as we raced through the deserted main street of the town.

We were free again.

But not because I'd killed Legs Diamond.

"What do you mean?" I asked Vinnie on the phone.

"It's okay," he said. "Somebody talked to the goons who scared your grandmother."

"What do you mean? Who? Talked to them about *what?*"

"About you and Dom."

"*Who* did?"

"Mickey Tataglia. He went to see them and convinced them you're not worth bothering with."

"But Diamond is dead. Why would they . . . ?"

"Yeah, somebody killed him, what a pity."

"So why would they be willing to forget . . . ?"

"Well, I think some money changed hands."

"How much money?"

"I don't know how much."

"You do know, Vinnie."

"I think maybe five thousand."

"Where'd the money come from?"

"I don't know."

"Whose money was it, Vinnie?"

The line went silent.

"Vinnie?"

More silence.

"Vinnie, was it Grandma's money? The money she's been saving for another shop?"

"I don't think it was her money. Let's just say somebody gave Mickey the money and he gave it to the goons, and you don't have to worry about anything anymore. Come on home."

"Who gave Mickey the money?"

"I have no idea. Come on home."

"*Whoever's* money it was, Vinnie . . . tell him I'll pay it all back one day."

"I'll tell him. Now come home, you and Dom."

"Vinnie?" I said. "Thank you very much."

"Come on, for what?" he said, and hung up.

When I told Dominique about the phone conversation, she said, "So you killed him for nothing."

I should have picked up on the word *you*.

But, after all, *she* hadn't killed anyone, had she?

"I killed him because I love you," I said.

"Alors, merci beaucoup," she said. "But money would have done it just as well, eh?"

A week after we got back to the city, Dominique told me that what we'd enjoyed together on the way to Chattanooga had been very nice, *bien sûr,* but she could never live with a man who had done murder, eh? However noble the cause. *En tout cas,* it was time she went back to Paris to make her home again in the land she loved.

"Tu comprends, mon cheri?" she said.

No, I wanted to say, I don't understand.

I thought we loved each other, I wanted to say.

That night on the train . . .

I thought it would last forever, you know?

I thought Legs Diamond would be our costar forever. We would run from him through all eternity, locked in embrace as he pursued us relentlessly and in vain. We would marry and we would have children and I would become rich and famous and Dominique would stay young and beautiful forever and our love would remain steadfast and true—but only because we would forever be running from Legs. That would be the steadily unifying force in our lives. Running from Legs.

We kissed good-bye.

We promised to stay in touch.

I never heard from her again.

Happy New Year, Herbie

We were living on North Brother Island at the time.

It was, and is, a tiny island in the middle of the East River, adjacent to a miniscule uninhabited island called South Brother. When we lived there, and I suppose the same is true of it now, the Riker's Island prison was visible in the distance from one end of the island, and from the opposite end, the Bronx mainland. There was a lot of river traffic passing North Brother. From our windows in one of the converted buildings we could see tugs and barges and transports and tankers and once even a Swedish luxury liner.

The buildings we lived in had once been part of a hospital for tuberculars, the hospital rooms converted into apartments shortly after the war. When Joan and I were first married, we lived in McCloskey Hall, which was on the end of the island opposite the tennis courts and the handball court and a sort of outdoor teahouse overlooking the edge of the river and Hell's Gate on the horizon. Later, just before our first son was born, we applied for and moved to a larger apartment on the other end of the island in a building called Finley Hall. If all of the buildings sounded like part of a college campus, it was with good reason. The island had initially been leased by Columbia, N.Y.U., and Fordham, I think, and was euphemistically called Riverside Campus or Riverside Extension or some such, the idea being to provide housing for World War II veterans who were attending these colleges. The unmarried students lived in a dormitory in the center of the island, the old administration building. The married veterans and their wives lived in the converted hospital buildings. Later on, the accommodations were extended to include veterans from other colleges in the city and, toward the end, the island accepted veterans who were attending *any* school approved by the Veterans Administration—which is how Herbie came to live on North Brother. I say "toward the end" not because the island went up in smoke or anything like that, but simply because the buildings eventually reverted to what they'd been originally: a hospital. In the old days, before the students invaded it, the island had housed such medical phenomena as Typhoid Mary. After we left, it became the Riverside Hospital for drug addicts. We, the interim students, were only a part of its brief, non-medical history.

Our apartment in Finley Hall was at the end of a long corridor on the fourth floor. The original hospital rooms had been revamped so that there were five apartments on each floor, the apartments varying in size according to the families occupying them. The smallest apartment on each floor was a single rectangular room that had once been the old hospital elevator shaft. On our floor it was shared by Peter, who was a dental student, and his wife Gerry, who listened to the radio wearing earphones so as not to disturb her husband while he studied.

Our own apartment was slightly larger than the converted elevator shaft. It consisted of two rooms and a john. The door opened on an enormous living room-dining room-kitchen combined, with windows facing the river north and south. Joan and I slept in the living room on a bed that doubled as a sofa during the day. The other room was smaller, with windows facing the river on the west, and Timmy—our newborn son—slept in that room. The bathroom was tacked onto one end of Timmy's room. We decorated the bathroom with covers from *Collier's* Magazine pasted to the wallboard, even though someone told us we'd lose our original security deposit if we papered the walls. But aside from this single effort, there wasn't much else we could do to improve the apartment. It had been hastily reconstructed in a time when new housing was practically nonexistent in New York. The paint was thin; the plasterboard showed through in uneven patches, and even the nails holding plasterboard to stud were clearly visible. The floors were presumably the original asphalt tile that had run through the old hospital. You could still see marks on the tile where entire walls had been ripped out in the transformation. The river moisture kept the apartment constantly damp, and the closed cupboards over the sink were a haven for cockroaches, no matter how many forays Joan and I made into their territory with insecticide powders and sprays. The view was magnificent, of course, and perhaps if we'd had any money we could have framed the view elegantly. But we were students living on my G.I. allotment and on what Joan and I could earn with part-time jobs.

Joan had dropped out of school just before Timmy was born, and I was in my senior year and working after school each day at the World Student Service Fund on West Fortieth Street and on Sundays at the Y as a counselor. On Saturdays, Joan went to her job in the music department at Macy's while I stayed home to wash and wax the old asphalt-tile floor, change Timmy's diapers, and continue my sworn and unceasing guerrilla warfare against the goddamn cockroaches. Joan had been a music major at Hunter College, which is how she'd got the job at Macy's. We'd been engaged for two years when we heard about North Brother Island and decided to get married immediately. I guess we'd both thought of marriage as having friends in for coffee, or of putting our laundry into a washing machine together, or of planning menus for the week. At least, our idea was to continue living in McCloskey Hall until we were both graduated and then go to Paris for a year where I would learn to write and Joan would continue with her studies at the Conservatory or someplace. But we were married in October, and on New Year's Eve of that first year on the island Timmy was conceived. And suddenly we were married in earnest and not on an extended honeymoon, and shortly after that we were parents to boot. It was our second New Year's Eve on the island, when we were living in Finley, that the thing happened with Herbie.

In a sense, despite our new responsibilities, our stay on the island *was* an extended honeymoon. We were surrounded by students or recent graduates who were just as broke as we were. The island was reached by a ferryboat that shuttled back and forth at unpredictable times, often carrying handcuffed convicts to Riker's Island as its second stop. There were hardly any automobiles on the island; you could walk from one end of it to the other in less than five minutes. On a still autumn night, even after Timmy was born, we would go outside with other married college students and play charades or even hide-and-seek. The island was peacefully quiet, and you could hear a baby if he so much as turned in his crib. On Sunday nights they would show old movies in the rec hall, stuff like *Citizen Kane* and *Pinocchio* and *The Philadelphia Story*. Admission was twenty-five cents a head, and Joan and I would take turns running up to check on Timmy every time the projectionist stopped to change a reel, unless we'd arranged for Peter and Gerry to look in on him. We used to keep our money in a little tin box divided into compartments, so much a week for rent, so much for transportation, so much for entertainment. I can remember a night when Joan wept herself to sleep because she'd backed a straight flush in a poker game and lost our three-dollar entertainment allotment to someone with a royal flush. The island was literally an island, but it was also a figurative never-never land that was a part of the city and yet removed from it. It was, in a sense, a country club for paupers.

Herbie moved into the apartment alongside ours just before Christmas. His wife's name was Shirley, and they had a son and a daughter, both under three years of age. Herbie was studying to be a television repairman. It is perhaps difficult to imagine snobbery among paupers, but the old-timers on the island strongly resented the new rules that allowed the admission of men going to upholstery schools, or television-repair schools, or even barbers' colleges. Many of the old island residents were men and women working for their master's degrees; some were going for their doctorates; most considered it beneath the dignity of the island to accept people who were not, by their standards, bona fide students. I wish I could say that Joan and I were unaffected by such petty considerations, but the truth is we felt as put upon as any of the others. The island was our neighborhood, our private retreat from the city. And now our neighborhood was getting run-down. We discussed it with our friends often and vehemently, and when Herbie and his wife moved into the apartment alongside ours and across the hall from Peter and Gerry, we unanimously felt there was now more to cope with than the indestructible cockroaches. And yet I don't think this resentment had anything to do with what happened on New Year's Eve. Or maybe it did; I simply don't know. I do know that Joan and I could have continued living on the island for many months after New Year's Eve and before it was reconverted to a hospital, but we applied for rooms in a city housing project instead. We left the island in March and never again saw any of the people who had been at the party that night.

I don't remember whose idea the party was. I think it was Jason's. It seems reasonable to assume this, because most of the ideas in Finley Hall, if not on the entire island, seemed to originate with Jason. I think he mentioned it casually just before Christmas while someone was serving eggnog laced with rum. I think it was only a drunken suggestion at first, "Let's have a New Year's Eve party," and then someone else said, "Why not?" and then Norman picked it up wholeheartedly—but yes, I'm sure the original suggestion was Jason's. And it must have been in his apartment at the other end of the fourth floor, facing inland, yes, and Mary had just put one of the kids to bed. They had at least a dozen kids in that small apartment. Well, actually they had only three, but even this was considerable when you realized Jason had only been out of Columbia for a year. He'd begun working at an advertising agency almost immediately upon graduation but was still taking some night courses, a dodge many of the married students used to maintain their eligibility for the low-rent island apartments. Mary didn't look like the mother of three children, or for that matter like the mother of even one child. In fact, Mary seemed to echo the fantasy that was North Brother Island, walking around with a three-year-old by her side, a two-year-old on her hip, and an infant in a carriage, and looking freckled and innocent and virginal in her sloppy sweaters and scuffed loafers, as if she had just wandered out of Julia Richman High School. Joan told me that Mary had called her to the window one afternoon shortly after we'd moved in, when Joan was in her eighth month and as big as a house, and had said, "Joan, will you come down and play with me?" She thought it odd that a woman with three children should be asking another grown woman—we all thought of ourselves as grownups then—to come down and play with her, but it seemed to me thoroughly appropriate for the woman who was married to Jason.

It was, in fact, impossible to imagine Jason in any conceivable world outside North Brother Island. The concept of him leaving the island to enter a city full of people earning their daily bread was almost laughable, and yet he did it every weekday morning, and with an earnestness that bordered on fanaticism. It was Jason who once leaped over the metal railing onto the deck of the ferry as it pulled away from the island. It was Jason who, on another morning, ran down to the dock in his pajamas, his working clothes slung over his arm, and then washed and dressed in the men's room before the boat reached the mainland. It was Jason who knew everyone on the island by his first name, Jason who first suggested we play hide-and-seek one night, Jason who discovered and used the outdoor barbecue near the teahouse looking out at Hell's Gate.

I had seen Jason often on the ferry while we were still living in McCloskey Hall. He was a tall, strikingly handsome man with black hair and blue eyes that seemed always smiling. His closest friend was a fellow named Norman who lived on the third floor of Finley Hall, a tall blond man with an excellent build and the same laughing look in his gray eyes. They would walk onto the ferry together, talking and joking, and then would go to sit in the bow of the boat where they were immediately surrounded by a half-dozen people who seemed to be having the time of their lives each morning. Sitting on the bench with an open book in my lap, hearing the sounds of laughter from the bow, I felt the unconscious pang of the outsider and longed for a moment to be a part of such obvious good fellowship.

I did not become a part of it until late August, when we had already moved into Finley Hall and were awaiting the birth of the baby. The first hurricane of the year came about three days before Joan expected to go to the hospital. I had been a New Yorker all my life and was used to the hurricane season, but I had never lived through a hurricane on an island in the middle of the East River with my wife momentarily expecting a baby. There was a cyclone fence around the entire island, and the water rose above that until the fence was no longer visible, and then the water covered the outdoor wash lines, and then it flooded into Finley Hall and began rising in the basement of the building. The radio was warning all residents of the city to tape windows and lash down any-thing that might be blown away, and the Coast Guard advised all residents of North Brother that it was standing by to take people to the mainland. The big question for everyone living in Finley, considering the fact that this was only the prelude to the storm, with the worst expected later in the afternoon, was whether or not to leave with the Coast Guard. The question was enormously magnified for me because I had visions of Joan suddenly going into labor at the height of the storm. We were debating whether or not to accept the Coast Guard's offer when we suddenly heard a drum beating somewhere in the building. We both went into the hall.

Jason was standing on the ground-floor landing, the water already up to his knees. He was wearing a yellow rubber rain cape and sou'wester, and he was beating a huge drum and shouting, "Hear ye, hear ye," while Norman read off a procla-mation. The proclamation stated that the residents of Finley Hall refused to be intimidated by the elements but instead chose to defend their homes in the teeth of the storm. It went on to imply strongly that anyone who left the building was, in effect, a rat deserting the sinking ship. There was, I must admit, an element of adventure to what Jason proposed. He wanted every able-bodied man to come immediately to the ground floor, where the furniture of the occupants there would be moved to a higher level just in case the water continued to rise. He then wanted a task force to go through the entire building, taping windows, making sure that cribs were protected from possible shattering glass, seeing that flashlights and kerosene lamps were available to each and every person who chose to remain.

I turned to Joan. "What do you think?" I asked.

There was a worried look on Joan's face. I now realize she was scared to death of having her first baby, terrified by the prospect of not being able to reach the hospital should she go into labor. I mistook her fear for the indecision of a nineteen-year-old. She turned to me; she turned to the strong guidance of her twenty-one-year-old husband. "Whatever you think," she said.

"Well, how do you feel?"

"I feel all right."

"Then let's stay, okay?"

Joan nodded doubtfully. "Okay," she said.

Under the leadership of Jason, we worked tirelessly all that afternoon, moving furniture, taping windows, and then sitting through the silence that came with the eye of the storm. The funny part was that the storm dissipated entirely. We were all awaiting the onslaught with a cheerful adventurousness that belied the actual danger. Looking from the fourth-floor window, it was impossible to tell where the island ended and the river began. Finley Hall rose like a tall white finger out of the waves, its basement and ground floor already flooded, the water halfway up the steps to the first floor. We had worked hard, and afterward Jason rewarded us with drinks in his apartment while we waited for the real storm to strike.

Instead, it blew out to sea.

170

I can still remember the slightly embarrassed faces of the people who had left the island and who returned the next morning, carrying their precious belongings. By then, I felt I was becoming one of Jason's friends, and I was able to share his laughter and his pointed gibes. The next day I took Joan to the hospital and Timmy was born.

I don't know how other people feel when they are presented with their first son. I now have three sons, and Timmy is almost thirteen years old, but I was twenty-one when he was born and a senior in college, and my pride at the time was mixed with a sense of unreality. I was a father; I could look through the plate-glass window at the hospital and see the red-faced infant they said was mine, but I honestly did not *feel* like a father. I felt instead as though I were only going through the time-honored motions of passing out cigars, of inviting Jason and Norman in for drinks, in an attempt to convince myself—without real conviction—that I was honestly a father. Jason, on the other hand, was my idea of what a parent should be. He was, after all, the father of three children, and yet he had never lost his youthfulness or his joy for living. I would watch him running through the hallway with his two eldest, firing toy guns at them, entering their world wholeheartedly, falling dead over the banister when one of his sons fired an imaginary bullet. I would watch him parading around the island with his infant daughter perched on his shoulders, pointing out the boats on the river, or the sunset, talking to her in a childish prattle that I'm sure to this day she understood. It seemed to me that this was the sort of relationship I wanted with my son. It seemed to me that Jason had managed to hang onto a marvelous capacity for finding fun in everything, and I was determined to follow his good example.

In October we had our Peeping Tom. In the middle of the night we heard a scream from the other end of the hallway, and then Jason was yelling something, and I leaped out of bed and ran to the door. Jason and Mary were already in the hallway, and Norman was running up from the third floor in his pajamas, shouting, "Jason? What is it? What's the matter?" Mary was wearing a baby-doll nightgown and no robe, but there was nothing provocative about her as she stood in the hallway behind Jason; she looked instead like a twelve-year-old who had been startled out of sleep by a bad dream. The dream, it seemed, was real enough. She had been nursing her daughter when she chanced to look up at the window and saw a man's face looking in at her. She had screamed and then covered her breast, and Jason had begun shouting at the man, and here we were now, standing in the chilly hallway in our pajamas, confronted with what looked like a very serious situation. We all knew there were unmarried students on the island, and it seemed to us now that one of them was possibly a pervert. It was four o'clock in the morning, and time for Timmy's bottle, so we all went into our apartment and Joan made some coffee while I warmed the bottle, and then while I fed Timmy we discussed what we were going to do about our Peeping Tom.

There was a feeling of warmth and unity in our kitchen that early morning, generated by the close friendship between Norman and Jason, the concern Norman showed for poor Mary. We sat drinking hot, steaming coffee, not at all frightened by what had happened to Mary, sweet Mary who looked like a high-school girl in her sweaters and skirts, but determined instead to find the intruder. We had no idea what we would do with him once we captured him, nor do I think any one of us was thinking in terms of punishment. The important thing was to catch him, and it became clear almost immediately that the chase, rather than the capture, would hold all the excitement.

There was no fire escape outside the window where the man's face had appeared. The windows on the inland side were high up on the wall, like elongated slits in a turret. Mary was sure the face had been hanging at her window upside down, so it seemed likely that the man had simply crawled to the edge of the roof and then leaned far out and over to peer in at her. To confirm our suspicions, Norman went for a flashlight, and we climbed the six steps from the fourth floor to the roof. We found that the lock on the roof door had been broken open. In our pajamas we walked to the edge of the roof directly above Mary's window. We found a discarded candy wrapper there, a sure sign to us that someone had recently been there.

Jason was bursting with plans. It never occurred to any of us to wonder how our Peeping Tom had known Mary would be nursing her baby at exactly four o'clock in the morning. We listened as Jason—who had been an ensign during the war —outlined a watch schedule for every man in Finley Hall on a rotating basis throughout the nights to follow. Norman loved the idea, and he devised an intricate alarm system, with each man in the building assigned a post to which he would hurry should our lookout sound the call.

We put the schedule into effect the following night.

There were twenty-two men living in Finley Hall at the time, five on each floor, and two on the ground-floor landing. We exempted from watch Peter, the dental student, because he was studying for exams—he was, it seemed to me, *always* studying for exams—and also a man named Mike on the second floor because he was holding a nighttime job as well as attending classes during the day. That left twenty men among whom to divide the ten P.M. to six A.M. watch schedule. We decided that a two-hour watch would be long enough for men who were expected to be bright and attentive the next morning. With twenty men available, this meant that each of us would stand watch once every five days. Actually I only got to stand two watches, one from midnight to two A.M., and the other from two A.M. to four A.M., before we called the whole thing off.

We never did catch our intruder; I'm not sure we were trying very hard. Besides, word of our vigilance spread all over the island, and our man would have been a fool to pay a return visit. But Jason's idea was a rewarding one nonetheless. We had all been subjected either to watches or guard duty during our time in the service, but this was somehow different. It was October, and not too cold, and there was something almost pioneerlike about setting the alarm and waking in the middle of the night, touching Joan's warm shoulder where she lay asleep in the sofa bed, and then going up to the roof where Norman was waiting to be relieved. Each night Mary provided a thermos of hot coffee for the men standing watch. Norman would hand over the flashlight, and I would pour myself a cup and then lean against the parapet wall, alone, looking up at the stars or out over the river. There was a lot of sky over North Brother Island. The stars were sharp and bright against it; the air was crisp. The factories on the mainland burned with activity all night, their long stacks sending up pillars of gray smoke tinted with the glow of neon. The prison on Riker's Island was dark except for probing fingers of light that occasionally pierced the blackness. There was hardly any river traffic, no hooting of tugs, no pounding diesels. Out on the dark water you could hear only the solemn gonging of the buoy marking South Brother Island and beneath that, if you listened very carefully, the gentle hiss of waves slipping almost soundlessly against the walls of the island.

I thought a lot of things alone on the roof of Finley Hall. I wondered about the future and about what was in store for Joan and me and our newborn son. I thought ahead to graduation; I thought of our canceled Paris sojourn, perhaps lost to us forever. I thought a lot about marriage and about what my responsibilities were supposed to be. The night encouraged speculation. I was twenty-one years old, and the world lay ahead of me, and I searched the darkness for answers it could not and did not contain.

That was in October.

In December, Herbie and Shirley and their two children moved into the building. I must describe them now as they first seemed to me and not as I came to see them later, after New Year's Eve. They were, to begin with, much older than most of the people on the island. Herbie was perhaps thirty-eight, and his wife was at least thirty-five. We were not still young enough to believe that anyone past thirty was middle-aged, but Herbie and Shirley were certainly beyond us in years, and this made them strangers to us. Then, too, they were from someplace in the Middle West; he had chosen to be discharged in New York City so that he could go to television school there before going back home with his family. So, in addition to their age, they spoke with an accent that was unfamiliar to most of us and grating on the ears. But, most important, Herbie and Shirley were not attractive people. He was short and stout and always seemed to have a beard stubble, even immediately after he had shaved. He was nearsighted and wore thick spectacles that magnified his eyes to almost Martian proportions. He was balding at the back of his head, unevenly, so that he always seemed in need of a haircut. He wore brown shoes with a blue suit, and he moved with a lumbering, ponderous gait that seemed designed to infuriate speedier people. His wife seemed to be a perfect soul mate. She called him "Herbert," and she looked at him with

175

adoring eyes that were a pale, washed-out blue in a shapeless plain face. She had borne two children and apparently never bothered with post-natal exercises; her figure, like her face, was shapeless, and she draped it with clothes in the poorest taste. She made only one concession to beauty, and that was in the form of a home bleach job on her hair, which left it looking like lifeless straw. Watching them walk to the ferry together was like watching a comic vaudeville routine. You always expected one or the other of them to take a pratfall, and when neither did, it only heightened their comic effect.

The walls on North Brother Island were hastily erected and paper-thin; Herbie and his wife lived in the apartment immediately next door to ours. It was impossible not to hear them in the middle of the night.

"Herbert," she would say, "do you think I'm beautiful?"

"I think you're very beautiful," Herbie would answer in his thick Midwestern voice.

"Do you think I have a good figure?"

"I think you have a beautiful figure, Shirley."

There would be a pause. Joan and I would lie motionless on our sofa bed. The night was still.

"Herbert, do you love me?"

"I love you, darling. I love you."

Joan got out of bed one night and whispered, "I don't want to listen. Please, do we have to listen?"

"Honey, what can we do?" I whispered back.

"I don't know. I'm going into Timmy's room. I don't want to listen. I think . . ." She shook her head. "It makes me feel that maybe we sound that way, too."

We went into Timmy's room. He was sleeping peacefully, his blond head turned into the pillow. We sat together in the old easy chair near his crib, Joan on my lap, her head on my shoulder. We sat quietly for a long time. The December winds raced over the river and shuddered against the windows in the small room.

Her mouth close to my ear, Joan whispered, "Are you very angry with me?"

"About what?"

"Paris. About not going."

"No," I said, but I suppose my voice could not hide my disappointment.

"I didn't want a baby so soon, you know," she said.

"I know, darling."

"But I do love him. He seems so helpless. Doesn't he seem helpless to you?"

"I suppose so."

"Do you wonder about us?" Joan asked.

"Sometimes."

"I do. A lot. I sometimes feel . . . I don't know . . . I feel we never talk to each other much any more, the way we used to when we were single." She paused. She was silent for a very long time. Then she said, "I don't want to get lost."

"We won't get lost."

"I don't want to get lost in people."

"We won't."

"I feel so . . . so terribly afraid that . . ." She shook her head.

"What is it, darling?"

"I have the feeling I never finished being a girl," she whispered, "and now I have to be a woman. I don't know what to do. Sometimes I feel like sitting on the dock where the ferry comes in and just let my feet hang in the water, and then I remember I'm a mother now and can't do that, but at the same time everything here seems so . . . as if, well, as if I could do that and nobody would mind very much or even notice it."

177

She paused again. "I'm going to say something terrible."

"What?"

"I wish we hadn't had the baby." She took a deep breath. "I wish we could have gone to Paris."

"We'll go one day," I whispered.

"Will it matter then?" she said, and she began weeping softly against my shoulder, and I could feel her trembling in my arms. In a little while we went back to bed. The apartment next door was silent.

My first real encounter with Herbie came shortly after Christmas. Joan's mother had given us a television set as a present, and I was busy at the pay telephone on the second-floor landing of Finley when Herbie came lumbering up the steps. I guess he couldn't help overhearing my conversation, which was with a television man, and which concerned the price of putting up an antenna and installing the set. He lingered awhile at the top of the landing, and when I hung up, he asked, "How much does he want?"

"Too much," I said.

Herbie smiled. There was a sweetness to his smile that contradicted his absurd appearance and his horrible speech. He offered his smile the way some men offer their hands for a handshake, openly and without guile.

"I'd be happy to do it for you," he said.

"What do you mean?"

"Put up the antenna, take care of the installation."

"Well, thanks," I said, "but I think . . ."

"I know how," Herbie said.

"Well, I'm sure you do, but . . ."

"I mean, in case you didn't think I knew how."

"I just wouldn't want to impose on your time, Herbie."

"Be no imposition at all. I'd be happy to do it."

I was trying to figure how I could possibly tell Herbie I would prefer paying for a professional job, even if it meant paying more than I would have to pay him for the installation, when he suddenly said, "I didn't mean to charge you, you know."

"What?"

"All you'd have to do would be pay for the parts, that's all. I'd be happy to put it up for the experience alone."

"Well . . ."

Herbie smiled gently. "None of us have too much money to throw around, I guess."

"I couldn't let you do that," I said.

"You'd be doing me a great favor," Herbie answered.

So that Saturday I went up to the roof with Herbie to put up the television antenna. It took me about five minutes to realize I wasn't needed at all, but I went on with the pretense of helping anyway, handing Herbie a tool every now and then, holding the antenna erect while he put the straps around the chimney, generally offering needless assistance. We'd been up there for about a half-hour when Jason and Norman joined us. They were both wearing old Navy foul-weather jackets, the wind whipping their hair into their eyes.

"Well, now, that's a pretty good job, Herbie," Jason said.

Herbie, tightening the wire straps around the chimney, smiled gently and said, "Thank you."

"How long have you been going to that school of yours?" Norman asked.

"Oh, just two months." Herbie shrugged apologetically. "This isn't too hard to learn, you know."

"Do you like doing it?" I asked.

"Oh, yes, I love it," Herbie said.

Jason looked at Norman with a smile on his face and then turned to Herbie again. "Were you involved with electronics

179

in the service?" he asked.

"Oh, no," Herbie said without looking up. He was retightening each wire strap until I felt sure the chimney brick would crumble. "I was a small-arms instructor at Fort Dix."

"That right?" Jason said, a curious lilt to his voice.

Herbie laughed. "I think I was taken by mistake. My eyes are terrible, you know."

"No!" Jason said, in mock surprise. "Your eyes? I don't believe it."

I looked at Jason curiously because I suddenly realized he was riding Herbie, and I couldn't see why, nor did I think it was very nice to ride a guy who was doing me a favor and saving me money. But Herbie didn't catch the inflection of Jason's voice. He went right on tightening the wire straps, and he laughed a little and said, "Oh, sure, I've been wearing these thick glasses ever since I was a kid. But, I don't know, the doctor who examined me said I was okay, so they drafted me." He shrugged. Cheerfully he added, "They used to call me Cockeye when I was a kid."

"How'd you like the Army?" I asked.

"I thought I was going to be a hero," Herbie said musingly. "Me, a hero. Wiping out German machine-gun nests, things like that, you know? Instead, the minute I got in, they took one look and realized just how blind I really was. They figured if they sent me over to fight, I'd be shooting at the wrong army all the time. So they made me an instructor." He shrugged. "After a while I began to enjoy it. I like taking things apart and putting them together again."

"Then television ought to be right up your alley," Jason said.

"Sure," Herbie agreed. He stepped back from the chimney and surveyed his work. "There, that ought to hold it. We get some pretty strong winds on this end of the island."

He walked away from the chimney and began paying out a roll of narrow wire to the edge of the roof. He worked with an intense concentration, a faint smile flickering on his mouth, as if he were pleased to see that things he'd learned in theory were actually capable of being put into practice.

"So you never got to be a hero, huh, Herbie?" Norman said, and his voice carried the same peculiar mocking tone as Jason's.

"I guess not," Herbie said, smiling. He shrugged. "But it's just a matter of coming to grips, isn't it?"

"Isn't *what?*" Norman said.

"All of it. All of life. Coming to grips, that's all." He shrugged. "When I was a kid, I used to cry in my pillow because they called me Cockeye. One night I threw my glasses on the floor and then stepped on them and broke them in a million pieces. Only that didn't change anything. I was still cockeyed in the morning, only worse because I didn't even have my glasses."

"I don't see what that has to do with being a hero," Jason said.

"Well, some guys never get to be heroes. I'm not so sure it's important."

"It might be," Jason said.

"You think so? I don't know. I keep asking myself what does Nappanee, Indiana, really need? A hero or a television repairman?" He grinned. "I think they need a television repairman."

"Maybe they need a hero, too," Jason said, and it suddenly seemed to me he was taking this all very personally, though I couldn't for the life of me see why.

"Maybe," Herbie admitted. "Listen, I think it would be very nice to be a television repairman and a hero. All I'm saying is that I'm happy to be what I am."

181

"Which is what, Herbie?"

Herbie looked up from the roll of wire, surprised, turning his face toward Jason. The glasses reflected the sky overhead, giving his eyes a curiously opaque look. "Why, *me,*" he said. "That's all. Me." He cocked his head and continued to look at Jason in puzzlement. "Look, I'm going to be cockeyed for the rest of my life, there's nothing going to change that. But I look at my kids' faces, I look into their eyes, I say to myself, Thank God, you've got good clear eyes and can see for twenty miles." He shrugged. "That's all."

"I think I'm missing your point, Herbie," Jason said.

"I'm not trying to make any point," Herbie said amiably. "I'm only saying that part of living is sooner or later you come to grips. You look around you and decide what's important, that's all. It's important to me that my kids have good eyes. That's more important to me than all the German machine-gun nests in the world." He walked to the edge of the roof and looked over. "Let's go down and hook this thing up, okay?" he said.

Jason hesitated a moment, glanced at Norman, and then smiled. "Herbie," he said slowly and evenly, "the tenants in the building are having a party on New Year's Eve. It'll be fun. Would you and Shirley like to come?"

Herbie turned from the edge of the roof. The sky was still reflected in his thick glasses, and the smile that covered his face was curiously eyeless. "We'd love to," he said softly. "Thank you very much."

I suppose the party began to go wrong while it was still in its planning stages, though none of us seemed to recognize it at the time. We were all living on very tight budgets, and whereas we wanted to have our party, we didn't want to have it at the expense of going hungry for the next month. It was decided almost immediately that everyone would bring his own bottle and that the party fund would provide setups. There was no disagreement on this point because it meant that each guest could bring and consume as much liquor as he desired without putting undue financial stress on the light drinkers in the building. Joan and I had hardly progressed beyond the two-drinks-an-evening stage of our social development, so we naturally were all for such an arrangement.

But all agreement seemed to end right there, and the party committee, of which I was a member, must have met at least four times between Christmas and New Year's Eve in an attempt to find a solution acceptable to all. The biggest areas of disagreement concerned food and decorations. There were members of the committee, and they presumably spoke for others in the building, who maintained that neither food nor decorations were necessary elements of a good party and that it would be foolish to waste money on them. The strongest proponent of this line of thought was Norman, whose wife was pregnant and who was undoubtedly trying to save every penny he could. If we'd gone along with his reasoning, the party would have cost him only the price of his own bottle, plus whatever we decided to chip in for setups. But Jason argued, with my firm support, that it wouldn't be New Year's Eve without food and balloons and confetti and noisemakers and hats. Norman countered by saying a good party was only a good collection of people, and Jason squelched him by suggesting we didn't even need liquor if a good party was only a good collection of people.

"We're paying for our *own* liquor!" Norman said heatedly.

"Yes, which is exactly why we should all chip in for decorations and food."

"No," Norman said. "In the first place . . ."

"Ah, come on, Norman," I put in. "If everyone drinks all

night without any food, we'll get sick."

"We'll get drunk," Norman said, "not *sick*."

"We've got to have *something* in our stomachs," Jason argued.

"Then eat *before* you come to the party!"

"The thing'll go on for hours. We're bound to get hungry again."

"Then bring your own food."

"That's ridiculous. It'll be cheaper if we all chip in for it."

"Why should we?" Norman said. "All I want to do is drink and celebrate New Year's Eve, so why should I chip in for food?"

"I think we ought to put it to a vote," Jason said.

We voted, and it was decided that each couple coming to the party would chip in five dollars for food, setups, and decorations. Norman was in a rage. He was Jason's closest friend, and this must have seemed like outright villainy to him. He had voted vehemently against the motion, and now he sulked in a corner for several moments and then said, "Well, *I'm* not chipping in for all that stuff."

"What do you mean?" Jason asked.

"Just what I said. If that's the price of admission, count me out."

"It's not the price of admission. We just want to make sure—"

"Then can I pay for the setups alone?"

"Well . . ."

"Oh, don't worry. I won't eat any of your food or touch your noisemakers or hats."

"You want me to lend you five dollars?" Jason asked.

"I don't need your five dollars, thanks. It's not the money, it's the principle."

"What are you going to do?" Jason asked. "Just sit there

with your wife while we all stuff ourselves?"

"We won't be hungry. We won't touch your food," Norman said with dignity.

With equal dignity Jason replied, "You are entirely welcome to come to the party, *and* to use our noisemakers and hats, *and* to eat our food. You are entirely welcome, Norman, whether you choose to pay the five dollars or not."

"If I don't pay, I won't eat," Norman said.

"And you won't make any noise, either, right?"

"I don't need noisemakers to make noise. God invented voices before he invented noisemakers."

"God invented tightwads, too, before he invented—"

"Now look, Jason," Norman said angrily, "don't go calling me a—"

"I apologize," Jason said angrily. "Are you coming to the party or not?"

"I'm coming to the party!" Norman shouted.

New Year's Eve that year was a cold and dismal night. The windowpanes in Timmy's room were frosted with ice, and we hung blankets over them to keep the cold away from his crib. Both Joan and I dressed in the kitchen near the radiator on the south wall. I wore my blue suit, and she put on the black dress she had worn to her college junior prom. I had mixed a plastic container full of orange juice and then poured some gin into it, and we expected that to last us the entire evening. We were about to go out of the apartment when Joan stopped me. She put her hands on my shoulders and reached up and very tenderly kissed me on the mouth and then whispered, "Happy new year, darling."

"It'll be a good year," I said, and Joan smiled and took my arm and we went out into the hallway. Herbie and Shirley were just coming out of their apartment next door. He was wearing a gray pin-stripe double-breasted suit that looked as if it had belonged to his father. Shirley was wearing black, and there was an orchid pinned to the waist of her dress. She smiled a bit shyly and said, "Herbert brings me an orchid every New Year's." Joan and I nodded in approval, and the four of us walked together to Jason's apartment at the end of the hall. The door was open, and the record player that Peter, the dental student, had provided was going full blast. We had worked in the apartment all that afternoon, moving furniture into the other room, leaving behind only chairs, a stand for the record player, and a long table, trying to clear the small room so that people could dance if they wanted to. Jason's three kids had been deposited in an apartment on the third floor—it would have been Norman's apartment had they not argued so vehemently before the party—and so were in no danger of being awakened by the revelries. We had strung crepe paper across the room and draped it with confetti streamers and balloons. Joan hadn't seen the results of our labor until we walked into the apartment, and she smiled now and squeezed my arm and said, "It looks marvelous."

There were perhaps twenty people in the apartment when we got there, with another ten expected, the rest of the tenants having made other plans for the night before the idea for the party presented itself. No one was dancing as yet, but there was a lively buzz in the room, and drinks were being poured freely, and the long table was set with the ham and turkey we'd bought, and several loaves of bread, and potato chips and pretzels, and celery and carrots, and it all looked very nice and warm and I began to have the feeling this was going to be one of the best New Year's Eves I'd ever spent. I poured drinks for Joan and myself from the plastic container, and then I set the container down on the table and asked Joan to dance, and Jason yelled, "There they go, they're breaking

the ice!" and everyone laughed. But we were indeed breaking
the ice, because Herbie and Shirley followed us onto the floor
almost immediately, and several other couples joined us, and
pretty soon everyone was dancing with the exception of Jason
and Mary, who stood in the doorway to the other room,
watching us with pleasant smiles on their faces, and Peter and
Gerry, who seemed to have discovered each other after a long
siege of struggling with teeth and were talking and laughing
as if they'd just been introduced. It took me several moments
to realize that Norman and his wife weren't in the room. I
looked at my watch. It was only ten-thirty, which wasn't too
late, considering this was New Year's Eve, but I began to
wonder whether or not Norman would show up. And then, as
if in answer to my question, Norman and his wife Alice
appeared in the doorway, smiling and carrying a bottle of
scotch, and they walked immediately to a pair of chairs opposite the long table set with food, far away from the table, clear
over on the other side of the room, and promptly poured
themselves drinks and began drinking.

"Well, let's eat," Jason said suddenly, and I turned to look
at him, because it was only ten-thirty, and many of the guests
hadn't shown up yet, and besides, most of us had had late
dinners in anticipation of the evening. But there he was,
moving toward the table and beginning to slice the ham.

"It's a little early, isn't it, Jason?" I said, smiling.

"I just want to keep up my strength," Jason answered.
"It's going to be a long night," and he continued to pile ham
and turkey into a sandwich and then bit into it hungrily and
smacked his lips and said, "Mmm, that's good," while
Norman watched him from the other side of the room with a
tight little smile on his mouth.

I don't think Norman or Alice budged from their chairs all
night long. They sat opposite the table piled with food, and

they made their keen displeasure felt by their presence, sitting like a pair of shocked chaperones witnessing an orgy. I didn't go near the table, and neither did a lot of other people, simply because Norman kept watching it with that small smile on his face, his eyes getting more and more glazed as he drank more and more Scotch. Jason, on the other hand, kept visiting the table as if it were a free lunch counter, eating like a glutton and smacking his lips with each bite he took, urging Mary to eat, pressing food on anyone who danced by, and then finally picking up the tray with the turkey on it and carrying it across the room to where Norman and Alice sat, getting quietly and angrily drunk.

"Won't you have some turkey, Norman?" he asked sweetly. "Alice?"

"Thank you, I'm not hungry," Norman said.

"It's eleven forty-five," Jason answered. "Come on, have a bite."

"Thank you," Alice said sweetly, "we had a late dinner."

"Why, Norman," Jason said, "you're not wearing a party hat. This is New Year's Eve. Mary, bring Norman a party hat."

"I don't need a party hat," Norman said.

"*Everybody* needs a party hat," Jason said.

"Not *me*," Norman answered firmly.

"Then have a balloon," Jason said, and he put the turkey tray down on a chair and reached up for a balloon and then suddenly pushed the balloon against the lighted end of Norman's cigarette. The balloon exploded, and Norman pulled back with a start and then leaped out of his chair, reached up for a balloon himself, held it close to Jason's face, and then touched it with his cigarette, exploding it. Jason laughed and reached for another balloon. Someone on the other side of the room, caught up in the excitement, pulled a balloon from the ceiling, dropped it to the floor, and stepped on it. And then someone else reached for a balloon, and before any of the dancers realized quite what was happening, the room was resounding with the noise of exploding balloons, and Jason and Norman were laughing hilariously.

"Oh, *get* me one, please," Joan said, "before they break them all. I want to give it to Timmy in the morning."

I reached up for a balloon and pulled it free and handed it to Joan, who began walking toward the bedroom with it, to put it on the bed for safekeeping. But Jason suddenly stepped into her path with a lighted cigarette and he thrust it at the balloon. Joan backed away from him, whirling so that the balloon was out of his reach.

"No!" she said, smiling. "I want this for my son."

But Jason lunged at the balloon again, and Norman came at her from the other side, as if all this explosive action had somehow washed away whatever ill feelings they were harboring, as if they were now united once more in having fun, the thing Jason knew how to lead best, the thing Norman knew how to follow.

"Stop it!" Joan said, holding the balloon high above her head, the smile no longer on her face. I started across the room toward her just as someone turned off the record player and turned on the radio. It was getting close to midnight, and the noise from Times Square was deafening, the announcer shouting over it in an attempt to describe the scene. Joan whirled again, but she was caught by Norman and Jason, who poked at the balloon with their cigarettes as I reached her side.

"Come on . . . ." I started to say, and suddenly Jason's cigarette touched the balloon and it exploded in Joan's face, and she said in a small, incredulous voice, "Oh, why'd you do that? I wanted it for my son," and then Jason and Norman

189

danced away from her, reaching up with their cigarettes to burst every balloon in the room, and suddenly the announcer was counting backward, ". . . nine, eight, seven, six, five, four, three, two, one . . ." and there was a pause, and he yelled, "Happy New Year! Happy New Year, everybody! It's a new *year*, everybody!" and the room went silent as we heard the words and turned to our wives.

I took Joan in my arms. I was surprised to feel tears on her face. I kissed her gently, and then I kissed her again, and then I simply held her in my arms and looked around the room where everyone was kissing his wife, and Joan whispered blankly, "I wanted it for Timmy," and suddenly Jason began laughing again and shouting, "Happy New Year! Happy New Year! Happ—"

His voice stopped abruptly. I turned to look at him and saw the grin starting on his face and then followed his gaze to where Herbie, lipstick-smeared, was moving away from Shirley. I smiled because I knew what Herbie was about to do. He was reaching for Mary's hand, and I knew he would kiss her for the new year, a custom we had always followed in my boyhood home, a custom we had followed at adolescent parties, and college parties, a custom that so far as I knew was followed everywhere in the world on New Year's Eve, even among young marrieds on North Brother Island. Grinning, Herbie reached over to kiss Mary on the cheek, and she pulled away from him.

I don't think he realized she was ducking his kiss at first. He thought, perhaps, that she didn't understand what he was trying to do, so he reached for her cheek with his lips again, and this time Mary giggled and definitely pulled away from him and said, "Oh, Herbie, *no!*" and I saw the puzzled look cross Herbie's face because he couldn't understand what was quite so objectionable. I had begun to shake my head, ready to tell Mary that all he wanted to do was kiss her for the new year, when suddenly I heard Jason's voice yelling, "Herbie wants to kiss the ladies!" and then Norman shouted, "Go ahead, Herbie, kiss all the ladies!"

Herbie stopped dead in the center of the room.

"Isn't . . ." He shrugged helplessly. "Back home, we . . ." He shrugged again.

"Sure, Herbie," Jason said, "go ahead, kiss them! Kiss them all! Mary, Herbie wants to kiss you!"

"No, that's all right," Herbie said. "You see, back home, it's what we . . ."

"*Kiss* him!" Jason said angrily, and he shoved Mary across the room and into Herbie's arms. Herbie was blushing now, a deep blush that started on his thick neck and worked its way over his face. He kissed Mary on the cheek quickly and then turned with one hand outstretched, embarrassed, reaching for the reassurance of his wife. But Jason yelled again, "That was fun! Kiss them all, Herbie!" and he grabbed Herbie's outstretched hand and dragged him across the room.

The room was silent now. Jason clung to Herbie's hand and led him from woman to woman as if he were forcing him to run a gantlet. With each kiss Herbie blushed more furiously. His eyes behind the thick glasses were blinking in confusion, as if he wondered how such a simple thing had suddenly become so monstrous. Beside me, I could feel Joan trembling. I watched in fascinated horror as Jason led Herbie around the room, holding his wrist tightly, shouting, "That was fun! Now the next one!" after each kiss. There were fourteen women besides Shirley in that room. The silence persisted as Herbie kissed each one of them. He turned away from the last woman in a blind sort of panic, searching for Shirley, seeing her, and then rushing across the room as Jason shouted, "How'd you like that, Herbie? You

191

like kissing the girls, huh?"

"*I* like kissing them, too," I said suddenly, surprised when the words came from my mouth. I squeezed Joan's hand quickly and briefly, and then I walked to where Shirley stood against the wall, her eyes frightened and confused, and I said, "Happy New Year, Shirley," and I kissed her gently on the cheek. I went around the silent room wishing each of the women a happy new year, and then I took Joan's hand, and I picked up the container of gin and orange juice, and I walked to the door and without turning I said, "Good night."

In the hallway Joan said, "I love you."

I didn't say anything. I felt as if I'd lost something in that apartment, and I didn't know what the hell it was. We undressed quietly. Before we got into bed, Joan said again, "I love you," and I nodded and turned my head into the pillow.

In a little while I heard the sound coming from the apartment next door. I got out of bed and walked to the wall. The sound was deep and soul-shattering, the sound of a grown man crying.

I stood near the wall listening, and then I bunched my fist and I banged it against the plasterboard, banged it with all my might, and I yelled, "Herbie!" as though I were yelling to a man who was drowning while I stood on the shore.

The sobbing stopped.

There was a silence.

"Yes?" Herbie answered in his thick Midwestern voice.

"Herbie," I yelled, "Happy New Year. You hear me, Herbie? Happy New Year!"

There was another silence.

Then Herbie said, "I hear you."

The Last Spin

The boy sitting opposite him was his enemy.

The boy sitting opposite him was called Tigo, and he wore a green silk jacket with an orange stripe on each sleeve. The jacket told Dave that Tigo was his enemy. The jacket shrieked "Enemy, enemy!"

"This is a good piece," Tigo said, indicating the gun on the table. "This runs you close to forty-five bucks, you try to buy it in a store."

The gun on the table was a Smith & Wesson .38 Police Special.

It rested exactly in the center of the table, its sawed-off two-inch barrel abruptly terminating the otherwise lethal grace of the weapon. There was a checked walnut stock on the gun, and the gun was finished in a flat blue. Alongside the gun were three .38 Special cartridges.

Dave looked at the gun disinterestedly. He was nervous and apprehensive, but he kept tight control of his face. He could not show Tigo what he was feeling. Tigo was the enemy, and so he presented a mask to the enemy, cocking one eyebrow and saying, "I seen pieces before. There's nothing special about this one."

"Except what we got to do with it," Tigo said. Tigo was studying him with large brown eyes. The eyes were moist-looking. He was not a bad-looking kid, Tigo, with thick black hair and maybe a nose that was too long, but his mouth and chin were good. You could usually tell a cat by his mouth and his chin. Tigo would not turkey out of this particular rumble. Of that, Dave was sure.

"Why don't we start?" Dave asked. He wet his lips and looked across at Tigo.

"You understand," Tigo said. "I got no bad blood for you."

"I understand."

"This is what the club said. This is how the club said we should settle it. Without a big street diddlebop, you dig? But I want you to know I don't know you from a hole in the wall— except you wear a blue and gold jacket."

"And you wear a green and orange one," Dave said, "and that's enough for me."

"Sure, but what I was trying to say . . ."

"We going to sit and talk all night, or we going to get this thing rolling?" Dave asked.

"What I'm trying to say," Tigo went on, "is that I just happened to be picked for this, you know? Like to settle this thing that's between the two clubs. I mean, you got to admit your boys shouldn't have come in our territory last night."

"I got to admit nothing," Dave said flatly.

"Well, anyway, they shot at the candy store. That wasn't right. There's supposed to be a truce on."

"Okay, okay," Dave said.

"So like . . . like this is the way we agreed to settle it. I mean, one of us and . . . and one of you. Fair and square. Without any street boppin', and without any law trouble."

"Let's get on with it," Dave said.

"I'm trying to say, I never even seen you on the street before this. So this ain't nothin' personal with me. Whichever way it turns out, like . . ."

"I never seen you neither," Dave said.

Tigo stared at him for a long time. "That's 'cause you're

new around here. Where you from originally?"

"My people come down from the Bronx."

"You got a big family?"

"A sister and two brothers, that's all."

"Yeah, I only got a sister," Tigo shrugged. "Well." He sighed. "So." He sighed again. "Let's make it, huh?"

"I'm waitin'," Dave said.

Tigo picked up the gun, and then he took one of the cartridges from the table top. He broke open the gun, slid the cartridge into the cylinder, and then snapped the gun shut and twirled the cylinder. "Round and round she goes," he said, "and where she stops, nobody knows. There's six chambers in the cylinder, and only one cartridge. That makes the odds five-to-one that the cartridge'll be in firing position when the cylinder stops twirling. You dig?"

"I dig."

"I'll go first," Tigo said.

Dave looked at him suspiciously. "Why?"

"You want to go first?"

"I don't know."

"I'm giving you a break." Tigo grinned. "I may blow my head off first time out."

"Why you giving me a break?" Dave asked.

Tigo shrugged. "What the hell's the difference?" He gave the cylinder a fast twirl.

"The Russians invented this, huh?" Dave asked.

"Yeah."

"I always said they was crazy bastards."

"Yeah, I always . . ." Tigo stopped talking. The cylinder was still now. He took a deep breath, put the barrel of the .38 to his temple, and then squeezed the trigger.

The firing pin clicked on an empty chamber.

"Well, that was easy, wasn't it?" he asked. He shoved the

gun across the table. "Your turn, Dave."

Dave reached for the gun. It was cold in the basement room, but he was sweating now. He pulled the gun toward him, then left it on the table while he dried his palms on his trousers. He picked up the gun then and stared at it.

"It's a nifty piece," Tigo said. "I like a good piece."

"Yeah, I do too," Dave said. "You can tell a good piece just by the way it feels in your hand."

Tigo looked surprised. "I mentioned that to one of the guys yesterday, and he thought I was nuts."

"Lots of guys don't know about pieces," Dave said, shrugging.

"I was thinking," Tigo said, "when I get old enough, I'll join the Army, you know? I'd like to work around pieces."

"I thought of that, too. I'd join now, only my old lady won't give me permission. She's got to sign if I join now."

"Yeah, they're all the same," Tigo said, smiling. "Your old lady born here or the island?"

"The island," Dave said.

"Yeah, well, you know they got these old-fashioned ideas."

"I better spin," Dave said.

"Yeah," Tigo agreed.

Dave slapped the cylinder with his left hand. The cylinder whirled, whirled and then stopped. Slowly, Dave put the gun to his head. He wanted to close his eyes, but he didn't dare. Tigo, the enemy, was watching him. He returned Tigo's stare, and then he squeezed the trigger.

His heart skipped a beat, and then over the roar of his blood he heard the empty click. Hastily, he put the gun down on the table.

"Makes you sweat, don't it?" Tigo said.

Dave nodded, saying nothing. He watched Tigo. Tigo

was looking at the gun.

"Me now, huh?" he said. He took a deep breath, then picked up the .38.

He shrugged. "Well." He twirled the cylinder, waited for it to stop, and then put the gun to his head.

"Bang!" he said, and then he squeezed the trigger. Again, the firing pin clicked on an empty chamber. Tigo let out his breath and put the gun down.

"I thought I was dead that time," he said.

"I could hear the harps," Dave said.

"This is a good way to lose weight, you know that?" He laughed nervously, and then his laugh became honest when he saw that Dave was laughing with him. "Ain't it the truth? You could lose ten pounds this way."

"My old lady's like a house," Dave said, laughing. "She ought to try this kind of a diet." He laughed at his own humor, pleased when Tigo joined him.

"That's the trouble," Tigo said. "You see a nice deb in the street, you think it's crazy, you know? Then they get to be our people's age, and they turn to fat." He shook his head.

"You got a chick?" Dave asked.

"Yeah, I got one."

"What's her name?"

"Aw, you don't know her."

"Maybe I do," Dave said.

"Her name is Juana." Tigo watched him. "She's about five-two, got these brown eyes . . ."

"I think I know her," Dave said. He nodded. "Yeah, I think I know her."

"She's nice, ain't she?" Tigo asked. He leaned forward, as if Dave's answer was of great importance to him.

"Yeah, she's nice," Dave said.

"The guys rib me about her. You know, all they're after—well, you know—they don't understand something like Juana."

"I got a chick, too," Dave said.

"Yeah? Hey, maybe sometime we could . . ." Tigo cut himself short. He looked down at the gun, and his sudden enthusiasm seemed to ebb completely. "It's your turn," he said.

"Here goes nothing," Dave said. He twirled the cylinder, sucked in his breath, and then fired.

The empty click was loud in the stillness of the room.

"Man!" Dave said.

"We're pretty lucky, you know?" Tigo said.

"So far."

"We better lower the odds. The boys won't like it if we . . ." He stopped himself again, and then reached for one of the cartridges on the table. He broke open the gun again, and slipped the second cartridge into the cylinder. "Now we got two cartridges in here," he said. "Two cartridges, six chambers. That's four-to-two. Divide it, and you get two-to-one." He paused. "You game?"

"That's . . . that's what we're here for, ain't it?"

"Sure."

"Okay then."

"Gone," Tigo said, nodding his head. "You got courage. Dave."

"You're the one needs the courage," Dave said gently. "It's your spin."

Tigo lifted the gun. Idly, he began spinning the cylinder.

"You live on the next block, don't you?" Dave asked.

"Yeah." Tigo kept slapping the cylinder. It spun with a gently whining sound.

"That's how come we never crossed paths, I guess. Also

198

I'm new on the scene."

"Yeah, well you know, you get hooked up with one club, that's the way it is."

"You like the guys on your club?" Dave asked, wondering why he was asking such a stupid question, listening to the whirring of the cylinder at the same time.

"They're okay." Tigo shrugged. "None of them really send me, but that's the club on my block, so what're you gonna do, huh?" His hand left the cylinder. It stopped spinning. He put the gun to his head.

"Wait!" Dave said.

Tigo looked puzzled. "What's the matter?"

"Nothing. I just wanted to say . . . I mean . . ." Dave frowned. "I don't dig too many of the guys on my club, either."

Tigo nodded. For a moment, their eyes locked. Then Tigo shrugged, and fired.

And the empty click filled the basement room.

"Phew," Tigo said.

"Man, you can say that again."

Tigo slid the gun across the table.

Dave hesitated an instant. He did not want to pick up the gun. He felt sure that this time the firing pin would strike the percussion cap of one of the cartridges. He was sure that this time he would shoot himself.

"Sometimes I think I'm turkey," he said to Tigo, surprised that his thoughts had found voice.

"I feel that way sometimes, too," Tigo said.

"I never told that to nobody," Dave said. "The guys on my club would laugh at me, I ever told them that."

"Some things you got to keep to yourself. There ain't nobody you can trust in this world."

"There should be somebody you can trust," Dave said.

"Hell, you can't tell nothing to your people. They don't understand."

Tigo laughed. "That's an old story. But that's the way things are. What're you gonna do?"

"Yeah. Still, sometimes I think I'm turkey."

"Sure, sure," Tigo said. "It ain't only that, though. Like sometimes . . . well, don't you wonder what you're doing stomping some guy in the street? Like . . . you know what I mean? Like . . . who's the guy to you? What you got to beat him up for? 'Cause he messed with somebody else's girl?" Tigo shook his head. "It gets complicated sometimes."

"Yeah, but . . ." Dave frowned again. "You got to stick with the club. Don't you?"

"Sure, sure . . . no question." Again, their eyes locked.

"Well, here goes," Dave said. He lifted the gun. "It's just . . ." He shook his head, and then twirled the cylinder. The cylinder spun, and then stopped. He studied the gun, wondering if one of the cartridges would roar from the barrel when he squeezed the trigger.

Then he fired.

Click.

"I didn't think you was going through with it," Tigo said.

"I didn't neither."

"You got heart, Dave," Tigo said. He looked at the gun. He picked it up and broke it open.

"What you doing?" Dave asked.

"Another cartridge," Tigo said. "Six chambers, *three* cartridges. That makes it even money. You game?"

"You?"

"The boys said . . ." Tigo stopped talking. "Yeah, I'm game," he added, his voice curiously low.

"It's your turn, you know."

"I know."

Dave watched as Tigo picked up the gun.

"You ever been rowboating on the lake?"

Tigo looked across the table at him, his eyes wide. "Once," he said. "I went with Juana."

"Is it . . . is it any kicks?"

"Yeah. Yeah, it's grand kicks. You mean you never been?"

"No," Dave said.

"Hey, you got to try it, man," Tigo said excitedly. "You'll like it. Hey, you try it."

"Yeah, I was thinking maybe this Sunday I'd . . ." He did not complete the sentence.

"My spin," Tigo said wearily. He twirled the cylinder. "Here goes a good man," he said, and he put the revolver to his head and squeezed the trigger.

Click.

Dave smiled nervously. "No rest for the weary," he said. "But, Jesus, you got heart. I don't know if I can go through with it."

"Sure, you can," Tigo assured him. "Listen, what's there to be afraid of?" He slid the gun across the table.

"We keep this up all night?" Dave asked.

"They said . . . you know . . ."

"Well, it ain't so bad. I mean, hell, we didn't have this operation, we wouldn'ta got a chance to talk, huh?" He grinned feebly.

"Yeah," Tigo said, his face splitting in a wide grin. "It ain't been so bad, huh?"

"No, it's been . . . well, you know, these guys on the club, who can talk to them?"

He picked up the gun.

"We could . . ." Tigo started.

"What?"

"We could say . . . well . . . like we kept shootin' an'

nothing happened, so . . ." Tigo shrugged. "What the hell! We can't do this all night, can we?"

"I don't know."

"Let's make this the last spin. Listen, they don't like it, they can take a flying leap, you know?"

"I don't think they'll like it. We supposed to settle this for the clubs."

"Screw the clubs!" Tigo said vehemently. "Can't we pick our own . . ." The word was hard coming. When it came, he said it softly, and his eyes did not leave Dave's face. ". . . friends?"

"Sure we can," Dave said fervently. "Sure we can! Why not?"

"The last spin," Tigo said. "Come on, the last spin."

"Gone," Dave said. "Hey, you know, I'm *glad* they got this idea. You know that? I'm actually glad!" He twirled the cylinder. "Look you want to go on the lake this Sunday? I mean, with your girl and mine? We could get two boats. Or even one if you want."

"Yeah, one boat," Tigo said. "Hey, your girl'll like Juana, I mean it. She's a swell chick."

The cylinder stopped. Dave put the gun to his head quickly.

"Here's to Sunday," he said. He grinned at Tigo, and Tigo grinned back, and then Dave fired.

The explosion rocked the small basement room, ripping away half of Dave's head, shattering his face. A small sharp cry escaped Tigo's throat, and a look of incredulous shock knifed his eyes. Then he put his head on the table and began weeping.